THE LUMBERJACKS' BALL

MACKINAC STRAITS LUMBERJACKS SERIES
Book 2

THE LUMBERJACKS' BALL

MACKINAC STRAITS LUMBERJACKS SERIES

Book 2

By

Carrie Fancett Pagels

Hearts Overcoming Press

First Edition, April 2015
Second Edition, November 2022

ISBN-13: 978-0692408513
ISBN-10: 0692408517

Hearts Overcoming Press
Printed and bound in the United States of America

Dedication

To my son,

Clark Jeffrey Pagels,

whom the Lord blessed me with,
fulfilling His promise to me.

Chapter One

St. Ignace, Michigan's Upper Peninsula, March 1891

White-wash, freshly sawn wood, and shellac vapors permeated the air inside the mercantile, encapsulating the scent of Rebecca's new beginning. Standing in the front center of the empty store, she clutched her blank order pad to her lace-covered chest. Outside the expanse of mullioned windows, an old carriage slowly churned its wheels through the slushy street. Across the roadway, the newest railroad tracks, all but unseen beneath clumps of dirty snow, ran parallel to the ferry docks. Beyond, the desolate white-capped waters of Lake Michigan churned dismal gray. If this was spring in the Upper Peninsula, then what would next winter be like?

The gusting wind swept through the cracks around the adjacent door. She shook off the sensation of abandonment that had swooped inside with it. Her parents had not left her alone since that fateful night a decade earlier. Finally, she was able to go about without her every move monitored. Her father's lack of protest had shocked her, other than his absurd comment when she'd insisted he returned home to have inventory shipped up from Lower Michigan. Rebecca had remained in the Upper Peninsula, a full-grown adult of twenty-seven years, finally treated like she had a mind of her own. *What a relief!*

Father had given her one month to hire a manager. "Or find a husband," he'd said. And he'd sounded serious! She laughed at the ridiculous comment. *As though I'd ever marry.* She had no intention of looking for either, since she was fully capable of running the new store herself.

Father knew her worth and must have enjoyed the jest he made. Her mother's "suffering" over the attempt made on her only daughter's life, must finally have worn as thin on her father as it had with her. Mother behaved as though she'd been the one left for dead, instead of the girl they once called "Janie," now identified by her first name, Rebecca.

A red-capped man strode determinedly down the boardwalk, his red-and-black-checked wool Mackinaw jacket marking him as a lumberjack. Her heart hammered as she stepped away from the window.

Hastily locking the door, she inhaled the scent of sawdust and swiveled around. Her footsteps echoed in the long rectangular room as she moved toward the back to examine the counter constructed by a local carpenter. She frowned. Such inferior work wouldn't stand the test of time.

The door rattled and she flinched. Rebecca turned to face the entrance, where a "shanty boy" stared through the window at her. Her breath caught in her throat as her heart betrayed her terror. The man's almost-black eyes shone against fair skin. A thick beard extended to the middle of his chest and a red wool Frenchman's cap covered his ebony hair.

Stop it right this minute! How will you ever be able to function on your own if you can't control your emotions?

The man attempted a smile, displaying a set of straight white teeth. He pointed to the door, but she remained frozen. Why hadn't she thought of this possibility? Why hadn't she considered that lumberjacks would call on her, at the mercantile, while she was alone—until Father returned or she found assistance?

Father had placed ads and she'd submitted another that morning. They'd already found a man to supply them with wood for the stove and to bring it in each morning. She doubted she'd see Mr. Carpenter, who made his rounds very early each day.

Rebecca closed her eyes and sent up a quick prayer as she prepared to unlock the entry.

C3⊗

Why wouldn't the woman open the door? Did he look that scary? Ox stroked his beard. Maybe it would be best to return when he'd had a shave and the owner was present.

He drew in a deep breath of frosty air and then exhaled, his breath fogging the window just as the woman finally headed toward the door.

Tall and slim, she moved with a natural grace constrained by tension, pulling at the fingers on her gloves, removing them as she approached the door and turned the latch.

The shop girl cracked the door open. A soft whoosh of warmth from the pot-bellied stove behind her flowed out.

"Good afternoon, miss. I'm here to ask about the cabinetry ad." He hoped the job hadn't been taken already; he sorely needed it if he was ever going to prove himself to his pa.

Ox pushed the door open as the woman stepped back, her mouth agape. Light brown hair, pulled back tightly from her face, strained her features, making them appear sharp in her creamy complexion. The hat squashed down over her hair did nothing to flatter her either. Wasn't that the point of a lady wearing those fussy little caps?

Even her dress was drab—a gray skirt and blouse. With no color on her person, she looked like she wanted to fade into the very new woodwork.

When she said nothing, he removed his wool cap and moved toward the stove. "Mighty chilly out there, miss."

She raised an ivory hand to her neck. "Aren't you a lumberjack?" Her voice was soft and low, stirring something in him.

Her hazel eyes appeared, somehow, familiar.

She took him for a lumberjack? True, he looked the part. But he'd not be a lumberjack much longer, if he had anything to say about it. Not if he could prove that he could build furniture. "Well, ma'am, I do work in a camp but I have some free time. And I'd like a chance to prove myself."

She arched a light brown eyebrow at him. "Prove?"

His cheeks heated. "I'm a good cabinet maker and I can do a sight better than what was done there, I reckon." He pointed to the counter that clearly had been slapped together.

"Can you bring me in a sample of your work?"

"Yes, ma'am, I'd be happy to." He'd bring the miniature cabinet he'd made as a wedding gift for his sister, Josephine.

"What hours are you available?" She ran a finger over the top of her shirt collar and frowned.

"I can get myself over here at night and after church on Sunday." He'd have to eat with Jo and her husband, Tom, at her bakery.

"I won't be here in the evening."

"No, ma'am, you shouldn't be." He looked around the wide room, noted the overpowering scent of fresh pine and shellac. Should have been applied elsewhere, not in the store. He nodded toward the front door and the docks of the wharf beyond. "You're too far down this here street from the main traffic."

The blush that bloomed on her face softened her features, making the woman appear almost pretty. *What in tarnation has gotten into me? Think about the job, man, not how fetching she is.* He shifted his weight. "I'd be happy to meet with your husband. I'm sure he'd not want his wife working down here at night."

Her high cheekbones reddened further. "I have no husband."

"Excuse me, ma'am. But may I meet with your father, then?"

She blinked rapidly. "No. You may return Sunday afternoon with your example." Her tone had turned icy as the straits of Mackinac.

3

Garrett recognized a dismissal when he heard one. "Thank you for the opportunity, ma'am."

She nodded curtly.

"Well, I'll be on my way, miss."

He stepped out into the frigid breeze; the lock clicked into place behind him. *Good.* That shop lady didn't need to be alone here. No husband. Her father not even there. Something in his spirit gave him pause. He headed to his sister's bakery. Maybe she and Tom could keep an eye on this single lady and make sure no one bothered her.

He slowed his steps and almost turned around. He'd failed to leave his name. With this move, he didn't need to be known as Ox—an ignorant but strong animal. His given name, Garrett, should be used. The Garrett of his youth was quiet, responsible, and half in love with a girl named Janie. *Why, after all these years, does that sweet gal come to mind?*

Now to get everyone to call him Garrett, not Ox. At least he didn't have the entire camp to contend with as far as correcting them. He groaned, pulled his cap down low over his ears, and bent his head against the wind. Instead of heading toward the bakery, he stopped in front of the barbershop.

His dark beard and Frenchman's cap reflected back at him in the glass window. What did his face look like now? The last time he'd seen his bare face, he'd been seventeen. After stopping Peevey's wicked plan, he'd no longer felt like a boy, but a man. Why, after all this time, did Janie come to mind? Perhaps because she, like this young woman, had a father who owned a mercantile. With waist-length golden blonde curls, Janie had always dressed fancy and seemed more like a decorative bird caged in her parents' store.

He opened the door and went inside. Another patron sat in the chair, a sheet wrapped around his thick neck. The barber brushed hair from the back of the man's head and collar then offered a mirror for inspection.

The barber turned to Garrett. "What can I do for you?"

"I'd like to take it all off." He made a circular motion over his long beard. Sometimes he felt as though he'd been trying to hide from God under all that bushy hair.

"Hope you got a lot of free time available, young man."

"Yes, sir." Garrett inhaled the mix of hair tonic, pipe, and wood smoke that hung in the air of the small square room.

Over an hour later, Garrett took a look in the mirror. The terrified boy's face he'd last seen beardless was gone, replaced by a man's firm, determined jaw. He stroked his smooth cheek and the cleft in his chin. After returning the mirror, he stood and dug coins from his pocket to pay the barber.

"Wonder what my sis is gonna say. She's not seen me beardless in so long, I reckon she might not recognize me."

"You got that right, son."

"Name's Garrett Christy." He thrust out his hand and they shook. "Thank you."

"If I didn't know any better, I'd think it was another man entirely who'll be walking out my door."

Laughing, Garrett nodded his goodbye and walked out, turning toward his sister's bakery.

Wait till Moose got a look at him—he wouldn't believe the difference, either. Janie, if she were here, she'd surely recognize him. Wouldn't she? He and Moose had vowed after Janie's rescue that they'd never leave their sister in a situation where someone could hurt her. And they'd lived up to that promise. Now, Jo was Tom's to protect.

But that woman in the new mercantile—who was watching over her?

Chapter Two

Standing in the woodworking shop behind the inn, Garrett blew sawdust from the area where he'd finished chiseling "Cordelia's Hotel" on the new sign. At least he wouldn't have to pull bits of wood from his now-missing beard. All he had to do was wash up. And with the innkeeper's insistence that he give up chewing tobacco, he'd have a cleaner face in general.

Cordelia Jeffries entered the small building, accompanied by the damp chill from the outside air. She crossed the rectangular room's plank floor and joined him. "Looks wonderful."

"Thank you. Just need to paint it." He grinned, pleased with the results. His skills could earn him compensation and would keep Pa from having to foot the bill for the inn.

Cordelia cocked her head. "Your sister suggested red and blue lettering against a white background and then black on the edges."

"Sounds good to me." Garrett wiped his hands on his work pants. He pointed to his row of paints, lined up neatly on the shelf he'd installed. "I bought those this morning."

"Very good." The lady patted his arm, bringing to mind the way his mother often had when she wanted to get his attention. A sharp pang of sadness shot through him.

"Glad you're happy, ma'am."

She smiled. "Jo tells me it's almost time for dinner to be served, and if you want any, you'd better come in."

His sister, Josephine, was set to wed Tom Jeffries the following summer. Slow business at her new bakery should pick up when tourist season began. In the meantime, she'd agreed to cook for her future mother-in-law's new hotel until full-time kitchen help was procured. For now, just Jo and three helpers ran the big kitchen. But the hotel currently only housed a dozen visitors.

"We have a new guest, too." Cordelia's smile widened. "The new general store owner."

"He's staying here?" Hadn't the young woman said he'd left?

The inn owner laughed. "*She* is staying here. And as I understand it, her father is one of those free-thinking men who believes women should be given their chance in business."

While Cordelia almost preened before him, happy in her cause for women's progress, Garrett cringed. The North Country was hardly a place for a lady, much less one on her own. This, at least, was a comfort to him though—she'd be at the hotel, surrounded by other people. And he could keep an eye on her like he used to do for Jo before she'd met Tom.

The image of a gaily dressed and laughing blonde girl danced though his mind. Janie.

"Anything wrong, Ox? You look like you've seen a ghost."

He sucked in a breath. "No. Just keep remembering someone from long ago." Someone he'd never forgotten—the girl responsible for his close guard over his sister, constant protective oversight that nearly cost Jo her happiness. "And if you don't mind, I'd prefer to be addressed by my given name, which is Garrett." He swallowed. This was going to take some getting used to.

She cocked her head. "Are you finally seeing how that moniker is demeaning?"

Moniker? He searched her face.

She must have noticed his confusion because she laughed. "Your nickname—Ox—means a big dumb animal. You are anything but that, young man."

"Thank you, ma'am. I'm honored to help you here at your new inn. We'll get the wainscoting and all looking just like you want it."

"Thank you, Garrett. And I want to tell you how pleased I am with everything you've built thus far, and how tidy you keep the woodworking shop." Her eyes lit with pleasure, spiraling approval through him, and he grinned back at her.

"Well, I'm sure you'll wish to tidy up before you join us at the table. Dinner will be served in half an hour."

"Yes, ma'am. I'll be there right quick once I've gussied myself up." He winked at her and she laughed then motioned for him to go on. What a nice treat to have indoor plumbing. And hot water in a real porcelain bathtub situated down the hallway from his room.

As he entered the hallway, the savory scents of roasted meat and something full of cinnamon greeted him. His mouth watered as he mounted the back stairwell up to his room. He made his way to the indoor bathroom to wash up. Too late for a bath, but he'd sure as shooting take one tonight after the ladies had tended to their needs.

Soon, he made his way back downstairs, this time descending the front staircase, which guests used. He eyed the empty stairwell's wall, absent a railing. He'd install one as soon as he could before somebody took a tumble.

As he approached the long walnut table in the hotel's private dining room, Cordelia gestured toward a young woman attired in pale gray finery. "Miss Hart, this is Garrett Christy, a talented woodworker, who is also staying at the hotel. You've met his sister, Jo, already."

Jo winked at him. "Garrett?"

"Just like Ma named me." He winked back at her.

Next, he met Miss Hart's wide eyes. "Garrett Christy?" she croaked. "Th…that was you earlier then, too?"

Her face blanched as she raised a hand to her high lace collar. To his surprise, she scooted her chair away from the table and rose. "Please excuse me. I'm feeling poorly."

Tom cocked his head at Garrett. "Seems you have quite the effect on women now that they can see your face, which I have to say is almost as good looking as mine."

"Thomas!" Cordelia scowled.

Jo laughed along with her fiancé, but Garrett didn't.

"You said her name was Miss Hart?"

Cordelia also rose from her chair and set her napkin back at its place. "Yes. Rebecca, the new proprietress of the mercantile."

Rebecca Hart. Daughter of the store owner. With hazel eyes that could look right into a man's soul, like Janie's. Garrett got to his feet as chills ran down his torso, almost feeling a cold, wet, and limp drowning girl pressed against him.

❦

Rebecca tried to catch her breath as she raised her skirts above her ankles and hurried upstairs to her room. Hot tears wet her face. *There's no getting away from my past.* No matter where she went she'd never be free. And with his newly bare face, she now had no doubt that this raven-haired man was the same handsome youth who'd saved her years earlier. And who'd given testimony at the trial.

"Stop!" A deep commanding voice with a Kentucky lilt sounded behind her.

Hesitating, one foot on the step above and the other below, Rebecca grasped for the handrail but finding no purchase, rested her palm against the wall.

"Don't run away from me, miss. I believe I know you." His steps moved closer and he grasped her elbow. "It's Miss Daggenhart, not Miss Hart, ain't it?"

She nodded slowly and felt the exhalation of his breath against her neck.

"I've never forgotten you, Janie. I've prayed for you all these years." His voice dropped into the bass register. "Please don't blame me for bringing up bad memories for you."

She drew in a slow breath and then exhaled, aware of his warm fingers on her arm. Heat from his broad chest emanated from close behind her. He pressed a handkerchief into her other hand.

"Please, come downstairs for dinner. It's some good victuals and I don't want ya to miss out. I'll make up a story about why you ran off from the table."

"I didn't run off," she huffed.

"If'n you say so, but it sure looked like it." He sighed. "Come back downstairs and eat up. No one but me knows who you are."

"Doesn't your sister know?"

"No." He barked out the word, then regretted his angry response and softened his words. "My parents wanted to protect her from any of those stories of what happened."

Some of the tightness in her shoulders eased. "And Mrs. Jeffries—does she know?" She sniffed.

"No."

Slowly she swiveled to face him. With Garrett a step behind her, she was now face-to-face with the handsome man. The gaslight reflected in his dark eyes. What she saw wasn't censure, ridicule, or accusation. She gazed into eyes filled with compassion that darkened when she remained fixed there.

Rosy patches shone on his cheeks as he averted his gaze. "Best be gettin' back downstairs, Janie." He turned, then stepped to the side to allow her to come down adjacent to him. Garrett slid his arm through hers, his knuckles brushing her waist, and she shivered.

"Garrett, I go by Rebecca Hart now, so please don't address me as Janie. Do you understand?"

He nodded. "Safer that way. Let me escort you to the dining room."

She moistened her lips as once again she drew near to the brightly lit dining chamber. The scent of roast pork, potatoes, and turnips mingled and appealed to her senses if not her intellect. The smartest thing would have been to continue up to her bedroom. Now, Garrett would have some explaining to do.

The others in the room quieted as they returned. What had they speculated?

Garrett pulled her chair out further for her and then pushed it beneath her voluminous skirts as she settled back in at her place. "I'm afraid Miss, um Hart, had the unfortunate situation of meeting me earlier at her new store when I was in my lumberjack gear. And I think seeing me without my beard has given her a bit of a shock."

"Indeed," Rebecca agreed, a smile tugging at her lips. She'd been more shocked to learn that the very man she needed to build her cabinetry was staying in the same hotel and was the one who'd made it possible for her to be there today, alive. But his presence reminded her that others might recognize her. *And know.* She didn't know if she could bear her new acquaintances learning of what had happened. She picked at some make-believe lint on her skirt.

"Well, then, let me commence with the prayer," Mrs. Jeffries suggested.

Jo, sitting adjacent to Rebecca, nudged her and whispered, "Yes, let's pray Garrett leaves that beard shaved off."

At that, Rebecca grinned and glanced shyly across the table. Dark penetrating eyes met hers as an ebony lock of hair fell across his brow. Yes, indeed, he needed to leave that beard off his handsome face.

∽∾

Sitting across the table, gazing at the now austere looking woman, Garrett drifted back to a summer night a decade earlier. He and his younger brother, Richard, had finished a happy day fishing for the plentiful and beautiful grayling fish in the AuSable River. They'd been preparing to return to camp after cooking some of their catch over the fire. They'd lingered far too late and the sun had already set when Garrett discerned the sound of a woman crying out—as though in pain. He'd told Richard to be still and to listen.

Thrashing sounds in the nearby dark woods, unlike those of moose or deer, was accompanied by a low, menacing male voice. Suspecting foul play, Garrett had doused their fire. Pa had instructed both of them on the dangers presented not only by animals but by some of the men in the rougher lumber camps. Pa had rejected many a shanty boy who had only whiskey, fighting, and women on their minds.

When a feminine shriek echoed through the woods, Richard tried to rise, but Garrett held him there for a moment, trying to get his bearings. The commotion was happening about thirty feet upriver from them, in the woods along the banks. Was it only one man or a gang of them? He crept closer to the edge of the clearing but couldn't hear anything. Soon, Richard joined him.

When the distinctive splash in the water occurred, both young men ran for the canoe, Garrett whispering to wait a moment before setting off.

Where the sandy point jutted out, the full moon reflected in the water, revealing the dark shape of a rail-thin man as he turned and headed back into the woods.

Richard scanned the silver moonlit path on the water.

Then he saw her.

"Get in!" he'd yelled to Richard, and they'd canoed out as fast as they could into the river's rapid current.

The still form in the water began to flail, moonlight glistening off the girl's blonde head as it bobbed above the water.

"God, help me!" she cried as they paddled toward her.

After maneuvering for the current, Richard held the canoe steady while Garrett pulled the soaked young woman into their boat, almost capsizing them in the process as she struggled.

"Help me," Janie had whimpered as she tugged at a rope still wrapped around her slender neck.

Careful to not rock the canoe further, Garrett untangled the cord and pulled it free, tossing it into the bottom of the boat.

"Thank you." The moon streamed down on the lovely face of the mercantile owner's daughter.

"Janie..." he'd whispered. "What happened?"

In the course of the upcoming weeks, when both he and his brother had to give testimony, Garrett heard what Myron Peevey had plotted against the pretty girl, who'd just attained her seventeenth birthday. Several years earlier, when Garrett's family had moved to the area, both he and Pa took note of the youth who trailed around after young, blonde Janie Daggenhart like a puppy. When they inquired about the odd Peevey boy, townspeople claimed he was Janie's friend. To learn what he'd done had sickened him. He and Richard determined to prevent Jo from ever suffering a similar fate.

He'd blamed himself for not running to Janie as soon as he'd heard the first cry. Should have grabbed Richard and then pummeled Peevey. What if he'd succeeded? Because of what happened, those dark memories propelled him past self-restraint and he'd begun reacting rather than thinking about, and being cautious, before responding to threats—especially where his own sister, Josephine, then fifteen, was concerned.

In a short time, he'd gone from Garrett, the boss's eldest son, to Ox, the young lumberjack who'd filled out, added eighty pounds of muscle, and couldn't be beaten at arm wrestling. As soon as Richard sprouted up, he'd been renamed Moose. The two brothers never let their sister out of sight.

Across the table Jo leaned in, whispering something to Janie that made her blush. Then she glanced at him. Was his sister talking about him?

Jo pushed a basket of fragrant hot rolls across the table to him and Tom. Her fiancé snatched them up first.

"Age before beauty, Ox," Tom said, before releasing them.

"Ox?" Miss Daggenhart arched an eyebrow at him.

He cleared his throat. "Yes'm, that's what they call me. What they used to." He shot a warning glance at Tom.

Josephine cast a glance at Janie. "Where are you from, Miss Hart?"

She began to gag on the tea she'd just raised to her mouth. When her choking spell stopped, she dabbed at her pink lips with the linen napkin. "All over Michigan." Then she stared downward at her china plate as though it was the most interesting specimen she'd yet seen of its kind.

Tom elbowed Garrett. "With as many relocations as the Christy lumber camp has had, I believe you could say the same thing."

For the meal's remainder, unease disturbed Garrett's enjoyment of the hearty fare. Eating in full view of the ladies slowed his intake. He wasn't performing a lumberjack's work right now, but his appetite hadn't yet matched up with his new activities. He'd helped the custodians chop wood, but no longer did he tramp out to the worksite and then back again to the camp.

After taking only one roll, which he lightly buttered, Garrett passed the basket to the two male boarders. The scruffier one, Harvey Sanders, scrutinized Jo with lascivious looks that previously would have earned him an escort away from the table by the Christy brothers. Tom eyed the admiring men, too, and then stole a look at Jo, who appeared unaware of the male attention she'd attracted.

His sister was a beautiful woman, there was no arguing that point. But as younger girls, Janie had outshone her—both in her dimpled smiles, her musical giggles, the elaborate hairstyles and ornamentation, and in the beautiful clothing she wore, down to her silver-buckled shoes. Now, Jo's fiery auburn radiance eclipsed "Rebecca's," who hid beneath her drab clothing and severe hairstyle as though in a shroud. What would it take to bring that laughing girl back to life again?

"You got a spittoon in here somewhere, ma'am?" Sanders asked.

Garrett stifled a laugh and instinctively felt in his pocket for his chaw. *Gone.* As was his usual inclination to correct someone's attitude by the use of his hands, he lightly clenched and released his hands, flummoxed that he didn't want to correct the stranger's assumption that he could spit in this lady's new inn. But hadn't he asked Cordelia the same thing?

The innkeeper batted her eyelashes at the fellow, and offered a tight smile. "Mr. Sanders, we don't allow tobacco in this establishment."

"Nor cussing," Tom added, wiping his mouth with the fancy napkin his mother always set out for them.

"Nor liquor." Jo raised her eyebrows at the light-haired man.

"Ma'am, with the cooking you have going on here, I won't need any of those vices." The new fellow grinned at Cordelia. "And the company here is wonderful, too."

When the boarder's eyes settled on Janie, Garrett's fists flexed of their own accord, and his heels dug into the oak floorboards beneath his feet as he prepared to push up. Tom grasped Garrett's shoulders, staying him.

"My future brother-in-law has been enjoying Jo's fine cooking for years, but I'm pleased to announce I'll be the recipient for the rest of my days." A muscle in Tom's cheek jumped.

Garrett almost chuckled. Tom must have thought Sanders was gawking at Josephine and not at Janie. Drawing in a slow breath, Garrett removed Tom's arm from his shoulder and rose from the table. "I'm gonna pour the coffee tonight, if you don't mind."

Janie peered up at him, her hazel eyes wide, and Cordelia did the same. "Why, Mr. Christy, thank you for your kindness to me and the staff."

Coffee was the one vice he was allowed. That and imagining himself holding Janie, rather Rebecca, in his arms—this time as a happy woman, and not the terrified girl he'd pulled from the river.

Chapter Three

More of Father's dusty old stock arrived daily, as well as dribs and drabs of items Rebecca had ordered. At this rate, she'd never gain clients, especially if she didn't bring in fresh goods. This sunny day, two carters bustled across Huron Street, from the railroad station and headed directly to her shop. A thrill of anticipation coursed through her as Rebecca opened the door for them. They grinned and pushed their loaded dollies up the walkway toward the mercantile.

"Missä haluat näitä laatikoita kyydistä, neiti?" The Finnish man from the dock spoke so rapidly, Rebecca had to consider the translation for a minute as she motioned him inside.

The other man, a younger blond who also appeared Finnish, followed the first into the almost empty room. He released the handles of his cart, straightened, and removed his hat. "Where you like them, miss?"

"Set the boxes here, please." She motioned for the workers from the wharf to set her new merchandise in the store's center.

The younger man removed his jacket and shoved his sleeves up. The odor of sardines clung to the two brawny men. Although she abhorred the fish, Rebecca carried the item in her shop, Father having ensured she received a case of his oldest tins.

The first man went back outside, ran across the street, and then returned with a tall barrel. *"Täällä?"* He set it down by the door and pointed.

The heavenly scent of apples emanated from the container. *Finally—fresh produce.*

"Kyllä, siellä, kiitos." How many times and in how many different languages had her father taught her those simple words—*yes, there, thanks*—before she'd mastered them? The younger man grinned at her.

"How much Finnish you know?"

"Just enough."

The man repeated her comment to the other Finlander and both men laughed. Rebecca plucked an apple from the barrel. Good color, lovely scent, and with a bite she savored the juicy fruit and affirmed the red Rome apple tasted delicious.

Once the porters completed depositing the cargo, she pressed several coins into their calloused hands.

"*Kiitos.*"

They departed and ran across the street, narrowly missing being trampled by a man on horseback. She shook her head as she watched. Hearing the back door open, she turned. She must have left it open, but she edged toward the front door, just in case…

Would Myron's attack forever loom in her mind? She couldn't panic every time a workman came to the back door. Her younger self would have bustled there to see who'd arrived, often to be gifted with a small whittled item, an especially pretty Petoskey stone, or a word of encouragement from the tradesmen. If it hadn't been for their kind attention after the attack, what would she have done these past ten years?

"*Hyvää huomenta,*" a stocky man called out.

Rebecca exhaled the breath she'd been holding. She better get used to all the Finnish men in these parts. "Good morning to you, too, Mr. Haavala."

He half pulled and half lifted a wooden structure into the store. She crossed the floorboards and stopped. The fisherman had asked her father for work. Before he'd departed for home, Father had tasked Mr. Haavala with the job of constructing a counter.

Rebecca scowled at the flimsy pine box cover with a foot-wide and seven-foot-long board. It reminded her of a coffin top. "That's your idea of a counter?"

"*Kyllä se on, neiti.*" He smelled of stale beer. At least she understood his words of affirmation, having picked up some basic phrases from several of the lumberjacks who had frequented her father's store. That had been before Father and Mother had kept her out of sight, in the back rooms.

"Well, it isn't my notion of one." She sighed in frustration but when he held out his dirty palm, she fished the money from her pouch and paid him. Father told her to make sure all workers were paid, and promptly.

"*Kiitos.*"

"You're welcome."

He nodded and turned to leave.

She called out, "*Älä vaivaudu tulossa takaisin.*"

The so-called-carpenter turned and raised an eyebrow. She nodded at him. "I mean it. Don't bother returning." Father hadn't said anything about not rehiring incompetent workers.

He pocketed his money, shrugged, and then left through the back. Rebecca placed her hand atop the plank, coming away with grit. The man hadn't even bothered using tack cloth to clean off the sawdust clinging to the board. And no doubt the sluggard would head down the street to the tavern.

When had she become so harsh? Rebecca crossed her arms as tears filled her eyes. She'd not become the woman she'd imagined she'd be—a kind and gracious lady, married, with a house full of children, engaged in church work. Myron Peevey hadn't killed her, not for a lack of trying, but he'd destroyed her dreams and that was almost as bad. A chill chased through her as she wiped her eyes dry.

The shop doorbell jingled and a nun, dressed in a black habit and matching wool cloak, accompanied by a pretty little girl of about ten years old, entered. The woman carried a placard, which she brought to the counter and set down.

"Lumberjacks' Ball" the sign proclaimed. But the date on the bottom was several months hence.

Rebecca cringed at the reminder that lumberjacks and lumber camps were all around the area. Myron had changed, became violent, once he'd run off to the lumber camps. She'd not had to work the front counter at her parents' store since the attack. She'd better accustom herself to waiting on them as well as the fishermen and merchants who populated St. Ignace.

"May I help you?"

The nun tapped a finger at the poster. "We sell crafts made by the orphans as a fundraiser at this event, but your competitor down the street won't extend us credit."

Rebecca cleared her throat. "I'm sorry, but I'm afraid we haven't met yet." She'd learned her lesson from the other day when she'd failed to ask Garrett, or "Ox," as he'd taken to calling himself, for his name.

"Oh, sorry, dearie, I'm Sister Mary Lou, and I'm at the convent down the street." The sweet-faced woman wrapped an arm around the girl, whose braids were so tight her hairline almost seemed to pucker. "This is Amelia."

The golden-haired girl bobbed a curtsey.

"I'm Rebecca...Hart, the new owner of the shop." She would be sole proprietress once she convinced her father. "My father has set me up in business here, but he's still my partner. He's given me discretion on extending credit, though."

The woman clapped her hands together. "Good. Because with donations decreasing for the orphanage, we've tapped out our account with Mr. Labron."

"I see. Well, why don't you sit down and tell me what you'll need." The only available seating was the two chairs recently delivered but as yet uncrated.

Her voice echoed in the almost empty room. Although crates were being moved in steadily by the men from the docks, she still had no display cases.

Sister Mary Lou and Amelia waited as Rebecca pulled the chairs free from the boxes and awkwardly sidled over to the counter with one chair at a time. The little girl sat on an overturned crate and pulled a tiny, blue, yarn doll from her pinafore pocket. A smile tugged at Rebecca's lips. How she'd loved playing with dolls as a girl, wishing one day she'd have her own children. But such was not to be. In a little over two years, she'd be thirty years old. She was unattached and had no intention of marrying. Why, then, did a certain tall, dark, and handsome lumberjack come to mind?

Focusing her attention to the task at hand, she sat beside Sister Mary Lou and opened her ledger.

"First of all, what is this Lumberjacks' Ball about?"

The little girl smiled shyly from where she sat. "That's where the shanty boys invite the town girls out to dance and celebrate the big haul being over."

"I see." Rebecca hadn't been to a dance since she was fourteen years old, and that was only because it was held in a family member's honor on Mackinac Island. She vaguely recollected there being a Woodsmen's Ball promoted about the time of her attack. "And do the girls have a gentleman invite them?"

The little girl nodded enthusiastically. "The lumberjacks ask the prettiest girls in town to go."

Rebecca felt her lips twitch. By no means would anyone find her attractive in her plain attire and severe hairstyle. And that was intentional.

Sister Mary Lou patted the child's hand. "We'll be making all kinds of goodies to sell that might help us keep food in the mouths of you orphans. That's what we need to focus on."

"Yes, Sister." The child lowered her head and began pulling bits of cloth from her pocket, which she used to "dress" her doll.

The pretty nun directed her attention to Rebecca. "I need ribbon, crochet hooks, yarn, knitting needles, and crochet thread."

"In what amounts?"

Sister Mary Lou opened a black satin reticule and, after retrieving a scrap of notepaper, pressed it into Rebecca's hands.

Rebecca felt her eyes widening as she scanned the numbers and the remainder of the list. Such goods would tap out a fair amount of her allocated credit budget at the Lumbermen's Bank down the street. "Am I correct in assuming you'd need to be advanced that full amount as a credit purchase?"

The nun's full lips thinned and she cast Rebecca a stern look.

"We might sell some of our popular antimacassars at one of our parish benefits before the dance. We could reimburse you with those receipts."

Rebecca tapped her pencil on the wooden countertop. "What level of return have you had on your previous attempts?"

"Five hundred percent." The nun's light eyes sparkled.

Great day! "You have yourself a deal, Sister." She laughed.

"Very good." The woman sighed. "Now, to keep little Amy here busy until the supplies arrive."

Glancing at all of her unopened boxes, an idea struck Rebecca. "Would Amelia be available to assist me in unpacking my inventory as it arrives? I can pay her from my budget and that cost can be either credited against your bill for supplies or used to purchase goods."

The two exchanged a quick glance and the child nodded enthusiastically. Sister Mary Lou patted Amelia's head. "If we might, I'd opt for using her wages toward extra canned goods for the children. Or fresh fruit if you get any in."

"I have oranges arriving soon. And we've got apples in the barrel by the door. They're delicious." She pointed to the remnants of her apple. "Help yourself. Could Amelia stay now?"

It would be much less lonely with the girl there. How had she in only a few short days gone from being ecstatic over her isolation to now craving company?

The nun's jaw dropped open as Rebecca pulled a large canvas bag from a crate and handed to her. "Fill that up. I'll have her back to you by dinner time."

"Very good. Thank you, dearie."

Amelia grinned and hopped up from her seat. "Do you have a hammer for me to uncrate these boxes, Miss Hart?"

"I do. And do you know how to use the nail puller to open them?"

"Yes, ma'am. Our supplies were always sent crated like this out to the island."

"Island?"

"Yes, ma'am. My parents owned a shop on Mackinac Island—until they took sick."

Rebecca didn't want to ask. If the child was at the orphanage, surely they had died. Amelia would discuss the details in her own good time. Why hadn't island residents taken the child into their home?

"I'm a little surprised the parish sent you over to the mainland, since Mackinac Island has their own orphanage at St. Anne's Church."

The child's lower lip began to quiver. "Sister Mary Lou asked for me to come."

"Oh?" Rebecca handed the child the hammer and the girl began to pry out the nails on the crate's lid.

"I tell you what, miss, I sure am glad I didn't have to stay over there anymore." Amelia's features hardened and for an instant she resembled an elderly woman.

"Were they unkind to you, then?"

"That ain't the half of it." Amelia opened the crate and began to lift items from the straw inside.

"I'm sorry." Horrible images danced through Rebecca's mind. "Did someone hurt you?"

"No, miss, but they yelled all the time and I wasn't used to that."

Sometimes Rebecca wished her parents had ranted and railed instead of discussing in hushed whispers and looking at her with disappointment, as though she'd brought Myron Peevey's attack upon herself. "Yes, well, I'm sure Sister Mary Lou doesn't yell."

"Nope. She's a real lady, but my dad would have said, 'she's a tough one.'"

"She'd have to be with all those orphans to look after."

"Yes, that's a true one if ever I heard it."

What must it be like with so many children to watch over? Perhaps Rebecca could volunteer to help, once she got the store up and running.

"Ooooh, that one is pretty!" Amelia pulled a white and pink rosebud teacup and saucer set free from its packaging. "Sister Mary Lou would love this set."

"It's beautiful, isn't it?" But where were the rest of the teacups she'd sent for?

The little girl ran her finger around the porcelain cup's rim. "When Lent is over, the parish is going to have a party for all the ladies who volunteered to help with us and with the church."

"Oh? That sounds very nice."

"Yes, it is." Amelia smiled up at her. "Maybe you'd like to donate something from your shop to it?"

The faintest twinge of offense plucked at her chest before Rebecca laughed. "I can tell you have the beginnings of a good little businesswoman."

"We always had people asking for donations on the island." The child set the teacup and saucer back in their wrappings. "What I don't understand is why with my parents being so kind, why didn't I receive that in return?"

"I can't say." Words filled her mouth and spilled forth, as though Rebecca could not contain them. "Sometimes what seems like something bad can become a blessing. We have to wait and pray to see what God does with this in your life."

Amelia's mouth fell open. "That is exactly what Father Paul told me last night."

And something God must have wanted the child to hear again. Rebecca pressed her fingertips to her lips, which tingled. Years had passed since God had given her a word to share with others. *A decade gone by.*

Whatever was within her power to show in kindness to this child, she would do. Rebecca pointed to the teacup set. "That's an early Easter gift for you, for being such a good helper."

"Really, Miss Hart?" Her eyes widened.

"Yes."

"Thank you." Amelia threw herself at Rebecca and hugged her tight. "I'm so glad I get to work for you!"

Blinking back moisture in her eyes, Rebecca patted the girl's back. "That makes two of us. Come back after school tomorrow."

Chapter Four

True to her word, Amelia returned the next afternoon. "It's sunny outside, today, Miss Hart, and Father Paul says the snow will soon melt away."

"Good day to you, too." Rebecca couldn't help but smile.

"Sorry, I should have said 'good afternoon' but I forgot—I'm so excited about working here."

"Hang up your coat." Rebecca almost called the child *sweetheart*, which her own mother had called her in front of customers. But only when others were present—why was she just now realizing that? The affectation had simply been for show. That realization stung.

"Yes, ma'am." Amelia hung her coat on a peg. "Can I look at my teacup?"

"After you've done your work, then you may."

The doorbells jingled as Garrett Christy entered, filling up the doorway. No wonder his comrades nicknamed him Ox. "I've brought something for you."

Exhaling loudly, Rebecca placed her hands on her aproned hips. "Good day to you, as well, Mr. Christy."

He frowned as his big hands clutched a dark-stained cherrywood box with drawers. It resembled a miniature display case. "Already wished you a good day this morning—don't that one still stand?"

Rebecca pressed her eyes closed for a moment. Between his grammatical issues and failure to maintain social etiquette, how would this man be a good example to little Amelia?

The orphan jumped up and ran to Mr. Christy. "Oh, it's beautiful, and I love the little heart."

"Thank you." The big man's cheeks reddened.

"I'm Amelia and I'll be helping here." She ran a finger over the heart. "Who is this for?"

"My name is Garrett Christy, and this here case is gonna be for someone real special."

Amelia turned to her. "Are you his sweetheart?"

Rebecca's jaw dropped, but she couldn't utter a word.

The girl glanced between the two of them. "Why, this is your wedding gift, isn't it, Miss Hart? A jewelry box to hold all the fine things that Mr. Christy will buy you someday, right? My mama had a case like this."

The lumberjack cleared his throat. "Actually, little gal, this here is an example of some display cabinets I'd like to build for Miss, um… Hart, who is fixing to be a fine businesswoman in this town, and far too good for the likes of a shanty boy like me."

With his eyes averted from her and fixed on the little girl, Rebecca furtively surveyed Garrett's handsome profile. Her breath caught in her throat. Did he truly believe she was too good for him? Or was he sparing her feelings by pretending?

Amelia bounced up and down, a gesture that reminded Rebecca of a very young Garrett when he'd accompanied his father to her store. "You should ask Miss Hart to the Lumberjacks' Ball before anyone else does."

Rebecca found her tongue. "Amelia, that's quite enough."

"Lumberjacks' Ball?" Garrett's dark eyebrows pulled together beneath the frayed cuff of his red Frenchman's cap. She'd give him one of the new ones as soon as they came in stock. Or had his true sweetheart, the one who'd attend the dance with him, knit the headcovering for him? If so, she'd only embarrass herself further if she offered him a store bought hat. *For pity's sake, he could be married already.*

"Mr. Christy surely already has a wife." His father always kept a family lumber camp. Surely at his age, and with him being the boss's son, he'd have married by now. She exhaled, certain he'd confirm her thoughts.

"Nope." He grinned lopsidedly and rocked back on his boot heels.

Clapping her tiny hands together, Amelia grinned. "Good—then you can ask Miss Hart."

"No!" they both shouted in unison.

The little girl's eyes filled with tears, and Rebecca wrapped an arm around her. "I'm sorry for yelling."

"Yeah, we didn't mean to scare you." Garrett bent down and touched the girl's chin.

The lumberjack's gesture bothered Rebecca and she pulled Amelia toward her. "And we weren't mad at you, child."

"Why did you shout then?" Her pink lips formed a pout.

"I, um…" She cast about for an answer, but could not explain her strong emotions to herself much less to a child.

When Garrett's eyes locked on hers, Rebecca's breath caught, for they held an open invitation despite his denial. And somehow, that pleased her.

If only her heart would stop galloping in her chest.

CREO

He might not be there in a few months, and Garrett wasn't about to be committing to attending any dances. Besides which, he didn't know how to do a jig unless one counted log rolling in the river as a dance. And the last time he'd tried inviting someone to the woodman's ball near camp—look how that turned out. His face heated in shame at the rejection he'd received. "I won't be going to the ball, little miss, that's why."

"Did you forget my name already?" She cocked her head at him. "You can call me Amy—it's easier to remember and I like it better."

He laughed. "No, I didn't forget your name little miss, Amy." He tweaked her pug nose.

She giggled. "You still didn't answer me. Why can't you go to the dance?"

"Aw, I'm kind of loud at celebrations, and that's not always appreciated by the womenfolk. I'm a big guy with a booming voice." That wasn't exactly true of him since he tried to keep his feelings, other than anger toward bullies, under control. If he wasn't protecting someone, he didn't have a loud voice. Who was he protecting now—Janie, whom he needed to think of as Rebecca, or himself?

"Neither will I be attending." Rebecca's pretty face became grim and Amy ducked behind her.

No surprise with Rebecca's pronouncement—she'd rejected his request those many years ago. Hadn't she? Sweat began to trickle down his collar.

"But let me see what you brought."

He set the example on her countertop. "You know I can fix you a better counter, too."

"Hmm?" Rebecca ran her finger slowly over the miniature cabinet's tiny shelves and then pulled a minuscule drawer open. "How did you make dovetail joints so small?"

He shrugged.

"This is exquisite." He heard her intake of breath before she looked up at him. And suddenly his lungs stopped working as he gazed into her hazel eyes and then down toward her lips. He broke his gaze away and stepped back.

"Thank you." He rubbed his chin, wishing he had his beard to cover his hot face, which always glowed red when he was embarrassed. Ma called it the mark of a true Irishman, those twin spots of red on his cheekbones when he was upset.

Amy peeked from behind Rebecca, eyes wide.

"How could we afford such expert craftsmanship?" Rebecca's stern voice would make her a formidable negotiator in a business deal.

"Well, I had some ideas about that." He had some notions he'd better control, too. "How about we discuss that over dinner tonight?"

"Miss Hart, I think Mr. Christy just asked you out for a social occasion." Amy slipped up and in between them, pulling at the drawers, open and shut.

"No, Amelia—so don't start any rumors." Rebecca dropped her chin. "Mr. Christy and I are staying at the same inn and we take our meals together at night."

"Oh." The child's forlorn tone tugged at his heart.

"I tell you what, though, Amy." He quirked an eyebrow at the little girl.

"What's that?"

He leaned in conspiratorially but whispered loudly enough so that Rebecca could hear, "If Miss Hart hires me then I'll be here a whole lot more. Maybe then you can teach me to dance better, little miss. Do you know how?"

The golden-haired girl bobbed a curtsey. "Yes, sir, I do."

He swept his hand through the air, in a pretense of a grand gesture. "There, you have it then."

When he turned to Rebecca, the film of tears in her eyes surprised him. Must be all the dust in the air from the crates.

"Miss Hart, what do you say? Do you need a good carpenter?"

ෂ𝓑𝓸

An acquaintance and almost-friend when they were young, her savior when older, and now a craftsman, Garrett Christy wanted to bring her store, her dream of freedom, to life. Rebecca quickly turned away from him, stifling a small sniff. "Yes," she called over her shoulder. "I'm going to the back for a moment."

Leaving Amelia with Garrett, she pulled her cloak from a peg and wrapped it around her shoulders and then went out the back door to the stoop. Nearby, daffodils pushed up through dark muck that passed for a minuscule garden. Had someone once lived on this property before the store had been built?

Across the alleyway, stacks of empty crates awaited either return to the wharf or breaking down into kindling by tobacconist who owned adjacent shop. Thank goodness Cordelia Jeffries had gotten Garrett to quit the nasty habit of chewing tobacco. It was hard to believe the well-muscled, broad-chested, and over six-foot-tall man was the lithe boy she'd known. Her closest "friend," or so she'd thought, had been Myron Peevey before he'd grown up and departed for the lumber camps closer to Traverse City. The

Christy brothers used to come to town weekly with their father, although rarely with their mother and sister. They'd always been kind and friendly to her, but she hadn't really known them.

She'd been seventeen when Myron suddenly turned on her. He'd arrived back from months at the camp and came to her house at early evening, tapping on her window, urging her to sneak out for a walk with him. He'd changed, she'd known it, since his father had died and he'd become a lumberjack with one of the most notorious camps in central Michigan. But somehow she'd believed that the young man, who'd practically worshipped her, was still that sweet, mistreated boy who'd followed her around. Instead, she'd been dragged to the AuSable River to die. Myron stuffed his filthy handkerchief in her mouth when she'd yelled but he'd pulled it out when she stopped struggling. He'd wrapped a rope around her neck and thrown it over an oak branch as she'd stared up, horrified, at the full moon. He'd intended to hang her and throw her body in the river. Myron pulled on the rope, lifting her feet from the ground, and she began to choke. If she had any chance of making it out of this alive, she had to do something. When the limb cracked and dropped, hitting her in the head, she fell to the ground and remained motionless—hoping he'd think she was dead. Or at least unconscious. With putrid breath, he'd bent over her, listening for her breathing. But then her once close friend lifted her body and she feigned limpness in his arms, once thin as rails but now as strong and unyielding as iron. Before he threw her in the water, she briefly opened her eyes and had spotted a flicker of light in the distance. She had drawn in the deepest breath she could. Then she floated, still, as the river carried her swiftly away. Lying on her back, she opened her eyes, gazing up at the stars in the sky and glanced toward shore where Myron disappeared into the thick woods. The swift water tugged at her clothing and she thrashed, pulling free her cloak. It drifted away from her as she moved downriver, water splashing in her face.

You are not alone. God's voice echoed in her heart.

I know, Lord, you are always with me. "God help me!" she cried out, fearing it might be her last utterance, when a pair of strong hands grasped her beneath her arms and hoisted her into a wobbling canoe as another young man worked to keep the vessel from flipping over.

Everything had happened so fast and she could barely see. "Who are you?" she'd rasped, her throat sore.

The one who had saved her removed the rope from her neck. "We're the Christy brothers."

When the full moon's light broke free again from the clouds, illuminating their faces, she'd realized that she knew them. They were the two handsome ebony-haired boys who liked to watch her from the corner of their dark eyes when they were in her father's store.

"You're not alone," her rescuer told her. "Not tonight. We've got you, miss, and we'll get you back to shore."

Chills, whether from the river or from Garrett Christy's words, the same as those whispered to her heart earlier, coursed through her. He'd wrapped a wool blanket around her. And that was to be the last warmth of genuine human kindness she'd experience. Until now. But could she trust that kindness?

Chapter Five

On her second week in the store, Rebecca arrived to find a drayman parked out front, and three crates leaned against the freshly painted building.

The driver tipped his black cap brim to her as he climbed up the side step and onto the dray's wide wooden seat. He pulled a fox fur across his lap and then a small bear hide. "Those crates are real lightweight, miss. Shouldn't be no trouble at all for you to bring 'em in."

Irritated, she glared up at the elderly man. Was this how men in the Upper Peninsula treated women?

Lifting the reins, his red bulging knuckles and misshapen fingers revealed the truth—he suffered from severe rheumatism. What was he doing driving a dray in this cold weather? And no gloves on. *Probably can't pull them over his fingers.* Sympathy mixed with guilt chased away her anger.

"Thank you, sir," she called out, and a smile tugged at his lips as he whistled for his horses and flicked the reins.

Soon she had the door unlocked and she slipped inside. After setting her pocketbook behind the counter, she went back outside to retrieve the boxes. As the carter had said, each of the upper two crates weighted so little that she easily carried them inside and set them by the east wall. But the third, which was longer, almost three feet across, was not only heavy but also cumbersome. She had to lift one end and drag the container into the store, her back pressed against the door until she got it inside, her heart beating with the effort.

"Lightweight. Humph! This one is heavy." She removed and hung up her blue wool coat and wool hat, and then tugged off her boots. Rebeca slipped her feet into a pair of navy leather pumps with shiny brass side buckles—the only bright ornamentation on any of her clothes.

First, she tended to the fire in the pot-bellied stove, then she decided to open the first shipment. What would it be? Too light to be the fabulous teacups and saucers that she'd ordered before she'd left. She lifted the uppermost container and set it on the floor, then pried the top free with a bar.

Rebecca lifted the bolt of raspberry moire silk satin from the crate and stared, trying to suppress her shock. Did Father really believe the local ladies of St. Ignace would have need of such a fancy fabric? That was the clientele they strove to reach, not the summer crowd of wealthy tourists. She frowned, trying to think of what the women had worn to church. She'd not noticed, spending most of her time aware of the man who sat beside her. Garrett seemed to fill up the entire pew even when more than six of them shared it. His presence monopolized her thoughts, and she'd struggled to focus on the sermon's message of Christ's provision in every circumstance.

In what instance would such fluffery as this fabric be used? She exhaled a puff of air and unrolled a yard of satin. It had a fine hand and was a perfect weight for a spring gown. She carried the cumbersome bolt to the Cheval mirror that Garrett had helped assemble, then unrolled enough yardage to drape the silk over her shoulder.

The bells over the door jingled as an elaborately dressed child entered. She took a second look. *Not a girl after all.* A tiny young woman, adorned in heavy black wool from head to toe, fixed a bright sapphire gaze on Rebecca. She wiped her heavy, leather boots on the new mat and stood there, clutching a rectangular pocketbook in her gloved hands.

"Good morning." When the petite woman remained near the door, Rebecca rolled the bolt of fabric back up and brought it to the counter.

"Could I...that is...the fabric you just put up—is it claimed?" The woman's voice was deeper, and warmer, than Rebecca anticipated, and held a note of authority despite the stutter in her words. Her boot heels clicked across the wood floor as she joined Rebecca at the counter and removed her gloves. She daintily stroked the rosy fabric. "It's so pretty. And I need a new gown made up for me. They don't have anything like this at Labrons."

That was the third time since she'd arrived that customers pointed out her competitor's store, at the other end of town.

"Take off your hat." Rebecca pointed to the nearby new oak hat rack that Garrett had built. "And let's see how this color goes with your hair."

"Oh." She patted the dark curls on her brow and then removed her heavy wool cap. "I'm afraid I usually pin my hair up so you won't see it well."

Didn't Rebecca do the same thing?

"I'm wanting a new dress for the Lumberjacks' Ball." The woman grinned shyly.

"Oh, yes, I've heard about that. So you've already been invited?"

The lady's cheeks flushed as bright as the cloth. "Not yet, but I'm praying Mr. Christy will invite me."

"Mr. Christy?" Sucking in a breath, Rebecca chose her next words carefully. "Oh, I see. Well, he's a very nice man."

"I know." She smiled prettily. "I'm Juliana Beauchamps, the librarian."

"Nice to meet you, Juliana. I'm Rebecca Hart, the proprietress of this mercantile." Garrett never mentioned visiting the library. How had the two met?

Rebecca wasn't Garrett Christy's keeper. And he'd done nothing to insinuate that she was anything more than someone offering him a craftsman's job; employment he wished to engage in far more than lumberjacking.

"You should come down to the library and get signed in as a patron. We have many good titles, despite our location."

The door swung open again and Amelia entered, pulling off a pair of red mittens. "Morning! How are you doing today?" She bobbed a curtsey to each woman.

Rebecca smiled at the little girl and motioned for her to come forward and hang her coat up. She held the satin across the librarian's narrow shoulders. "Doesn't this color look lovely on Miss Beauchamps?"

Perfectly wonderful—the rosy hue brought out the pink in her cheeks and the blue of her eyes. Garrett should be impressed with the result. What a handsome couple they would make. But that image was quickly erased by a picture of her and Garrett, her arm interlocked with his, entering the dance, laughing.

"Rebecca, are you all right?" Sapphire eyes met hers.

"Yes." She forced a smile. "Have you met Amelia? She's my new helper."

"Indeed, the children from the orphanage come regularly to pick out the books they wish to read. And Amy likes Louisa May Alcott's books best, don't you?"

"Yes, ma'am."

"And the fashion books, too. Am I right?" Juliana smiled benevolently at the girl, who stood only inches shorter than she did.

"I do, ma'am, but I'm not so good at stitching." She dropped her blonde head and then looked up from beneath golden eyelashes. "Sister Mary Lou could sew you up a really pretty dress—that's her hobby when she's not watching us kids."

"Is that so?" The other woman's blue eyes sparkled. "I wonder how many yards I need?"

Amelia went to the crate that held the rest of the cloth. "Have you looked at these other fabrics? This is the prettiest cloth I've seen around here."

Juliana followed Rebecca and they bent over the assortment.

Running her hand along the bolts, Rebecca quickly checked for matching fabric. "I'm afraid I don't see more of the raspberry silk, but I think you'll have plenty on that one bolt because it's full."

Amelia pulled out mossy crushed velvet from the collection. "What about this emerald color for you, Miss Hart? It brings out your hazel eyes."

Rebecca cringed. She didn't want anything bringing attention to her—not to her eyes nor to anything on her person. She returned to the counter, leaving the librarian and Amelia "oohing" and "ahing" over the fabrics.

One person came to mind, whom she would like to notice her. But how would that be possible? Garrett would remind her of that awful episode every time she looked at him. But she'd schooled herself now to not gaze at him, because although he did, indeed, bring back painful memories, he also called up feelings in her that she dare not recognize. She cast a glance at the petite local woman who had set her sights on the man who'd saved Rebecca's life. An ache began somewhere deep inside her and her eyes moistened.

Amelia touched the librarian's tightly coiled bun. "I bet your hair is as pretty as my mother's if you'd let it down and curl it."

With two flicks of her wrist, the child had the pins pulled free and dark locks tumbled down Juliana's back like a gorgeous waterfall.

An early spring breeze announced Garrett as he entered the room. Rebecca had no right to feel jealous, but she did. And there was little point in lying to herself.

છ8ல

"Good morning, ladies." He winked at Amy, who bobbed him a curtsy. Then he laughed at the sight of the girl performing such a gesture in an almost empty storeroom with sawdust still liberally sprinkled across the floor. The other workers hadn't cleaned up after themselves, like he had. And if Janie was holding her breath thinking they'd be back to do so, she'd be dead soon from lack of air. He'd take care of it himself later, when she went for lunch.

With care, he strode forward, trying to not kick up the dust.

"Good day, Mr. Christy," Rebecca addressed him, but her features pinched as though she'd caught a whiff of polecat.

"Mr. *Christy*?" The tiny gal, dressed in mourning, rapidly blinked her large blue eyes. "Are you related to the *other* Mr. Christy?"

He stopped walking. He'd not seen Moose in town since they'd arrived. He was supposed to be taking care of their pa's business at the new site.

The little woman rose up on tiptoe in her ugly black boots and held her gloved hands high. "Even taller than you?"

A flush began to heat beneath his red-and-black flannel shirt as he unbuttoned his wool overcoat, turned his back to them, and then hung it on a wood peg he'd hammered in the wall yesterday. Even when they were much younger, people mistook Richard's height to mean he was the older brother. That had constantly grated on Garrett until he'd grown a beard and his younger brother hadn't been able to do so.

"Yes, ma'am, I'm his older and better-looking brother." He'd started making this joke in camp and the other lumberjacks got a kick out of it.

But when he'd turned around, Rebecca wore a look of disapproval. The shorter lady cocked her head at him. Only the child laughed, covering her mouth with her hand.

He shrugged. "Just a joke, but yes, he's my brother."

"He's here, too?" Rebecca's strained voice was just above a whisper. Did his employer harbor some secret feelings toward his brother, other than gratitude?

The little lady clasped her hands together and smiled. "I met him at the library just this morning."

"This morning?" Both he and Rebecca uttered the words simultaneously and her eyebrows raised as high as his must be.

With crimson creeping up from her high collar, the woman placed a hand near her neck and nodded. "Yes, well, I really have to get back to the library. I just wanted to look at some fabric for a dress."

Amy bobbed on her tiptoes. "She's making a dress for—"

"Amelia!" Rebecca's curt tone cut the girl's words off. Both women wore the same expression the lumberjacks wore when they saw a tree coming down and someone beneath it who needed to get out of the way fast.

He stroked his chin, not liking the way this conversation was going. "I'm here to get started on those cabinets, Miss Hart."

"Come on through then, Mr. Christy." Rebecca's clipped tone propelled him toward the back.

The librarian offered him a shy smile as he passed, making his way around the shoddy counter to the back. He closed the makeshift curtain, a long piece of dun-colored fabric, as he passed through. Sniffing the scent of new wood appreciatively, he strode to his worktable and set out his tools. He needed to examine the wood delivered from the mill the previous day, when he'd gone out to purchase more sandpaper. As he crossed the plank floor to look at the new boards, he spied a clump of tobacco on the floor that he'd swept clean from his previous day's work. *Darned fools.* Who had been smoking in here? Next time, if he left the store and returned, he'd be sure to come around to the back and check before he walked Rebecca to the inn. And someone should have a word with the lumberyard manager about his *no account* helpers. Garrett grabbed the broom and dustpan and swept up the tobacco then tossed it in the trash bin.

Some people are so careless. His shoulders stiffened. Since he'd been released from his own self-assigned supervision of Jo, he'd been freed of his daily watch over her. Looking after Rebecca didn't tax him as much—not like it did keeping the lumberjacks away from his sister. On the other hand, one Myron Peevey was more dangerous than a Christy lumber camp full of shanty boys.

Chapter Six

Garrett slowly ate his breakfast, trying to keep the turtle pace that Rebecca set. He'd never seen a young woman look so pretty first thing in the morning as she did. What would it be like to wake up to a wife so lovely? Even in the drab clothing she'd donned this day, Rebecca still shone like a jewel, illuminated by the rays piercing the nearby parted drapes. But she deserved better treatment than she gave herself.

"You seem lost in thought, Mr. Christy." Rebecca eyed him, holding a forkful of ham, which she brought to those wide, pink lips of hers.

If she donned a new frock for Easter, she would, at least for one day, seem bright and new and not this diluted version of the girl he knew. He'd talk to Cordelia, or maybe little Amy, and see what they could do, or better yet, Jo.

"I was thinking about Easter coming up next week."

She dabbed her mouth with her napkin. "Oh dear, with all the work at the store I'd almost forgotten."

Jo carried a silver tray, piled with biscuits, into the room. "What have you forgotten?"

"Easter," he and Rebecca said.

"How could you overlook the most important day of the year for Christians?"

Rebecca locked eyes with him. "The store has distracted me."

Jo slid into a chair. "I've been stitching up a lemon-yellow skirt so I'll have something new. And I made Tom a matching handkerchief for his suit pocket. I love Easter. It's like the chance to start all over again—reminded by what Christ did for us on the cross to cleanse us of our sins."

Her words stirred discomfort. Did Christ die to save men like Myron Peevey, too? Didn't seem right. On the other hand, if he'd gotten religion in the penitentiary then maybe there was some hope they'd never see him again in this lifetime.

"Only time of year I let Ma dress me up, but this year I reckon I'll have to…" He was about to say "make do" but caught himself. "I'll need to stop by Labrons and get me some new clothes. Maybe Rebecca would like to come with me."

Jo nodded. "Their ready-made items are good quality. I don't think you'd have time to have something made for you before next week, Rebecca."

"Right, but I have plenty of serviceable clothes. I can't see what making a fuss over a fancy new outfit will do for my appreciation of Easter." Rebecca scooted back and Garrett followed her cue. "I need to get to work."

"Mind if I accompany you?"

Rebecca shrugged.

His sister's face reflected her hurt over Rebecca's harsh comment. She stood. "You know, Miss Hart, that you, of anyone, should know how something new and bright can lift one's spirits. After all, your shop carries many pretty items. Yet you attire yourself as plainly as possible."

Oh no, Jo's on a roll. In a moment, both women might be pushing up their sleeves to do battle. "Why I reckon that's because, good businesswoman that she is, Miss Hart doesn't want to detract from her inventory. Ain't that right?"

Rebecca's hands were clasped so tightly together that the knuckles almost glowed white. She released them and removed her coat from the nearby rack. "You both make good points that I shall take under consideration as I replace my wardrobe this spring."

"I'll help you when you do, and the two of you have a good day."

"Thank you. I must get going back to the mercantile."

"Once I've finished helping here, I'll be off to my bakery." Jo clapped her hands together and beamed at them. "It sounds so good to be able to call it my own place—a dream come true. But right now I better head off to the kitchen."

"Bring us cookies later," Garrett called as she walked down the hall.

Jo raised a hand, dismissing him.

"Don't count on that." Rebecca strode toward the front door.

They exited out into a cool day, the sky a brilliant blue behind the morning mist.

"Would you like to sit in our pew on Easter Sunday?"

She grimaced. "Don't I sit there with you now?"

"Yes, but…" This was different. This was how family sat for holidays. And he wanted her with them.

Stopping, she caught his arm. "I'll find something to wear that will be cheerful and new and I won't distract from the gaily attired people in your pew, if that is what's worrying you."

"No."

They resumed walking, in silence until they reached the mercantile. "Here we are."

Once inside, he took her elbow. "It's not my place to say, but I feel like you're hiding who you really are. Not just with your name but by…" He gestured from head to toe.

She pulled away. "You're right, Mr. Christy. It's not your place to say."

He swallowed hard and tried to assist her in removing her coat, but she shrugged away. He'd pushed too hard. Would need to back away and give her time to consider. "I'm gonna go fashion that wardrobe you wanted."

"Good."

That day he worked until he'd completed the basic structure that Rebecca wanted. The armoire would display ready-made dresses, which should be arriving within the week from her father. Another carpenter had delivered a long table for stacking fabric, but no boards were affixed to the sides to contain the material in case it shifted. Disgusted that she had received more poor workmanship, Garrett decided to add a second level to the table and adorn both layers with a scalloped edge.

C�O

All day long, Rebecca fought the agitation that the morning's conversation had stirred in her spirit. Every time she glanced toward the back, she wanted to go to Garrett and apologize for her surly behavior. But she couldn't. Because these strong emotions rolling over her needed to be released. Time had come for her to face her demons and drive them out.

When Amelia arrived, she first gave Rebecca a quick hug and then ran to the back to do the same with Garrett. Almost as if they were a little family. The gesture both warmed and unnerved her. She returned to the front and began to dust the shelves.

Jingling bells announced the librarian's arrival. The tiny dark-haired woman hurried toward her. "How are you Juliana?"

"I'm ever so fine, how are you?" She clasped her white-gloved hands together and raised them to her cheek. "I just saw my Mr. Christy, again."

Her Mr. Christy? Was she implying that Garrett was Rebecca's Mr. Christy? "You did?"

"Yes, and I think he's invited me to attend Easter service with him."

"Oh." So it really wasn't that special that Garrett had asked her.

"At least I think he asked me." Juliana's dark eyebrows pulled together. "He stopped by the library to get a book. Then he said he was looking forward to going to church on Easter. And then he gazed right at me for what seemed like a full minute."

The young woman's romantic enthusiasm should stir something in Rebecca but confusion kept her from encouraging her. "And what did you say to him?"

"I couldn't say anything, my supervisor came up and librarians are not allowed to be having private conversations with the clients. Particularly *not* single librarians and young men."

Biting her tongue, Rebecca refrained from suggesting that Richard may have been trying to determine if she held his same faith. Or he may simply have been making conversation.

"So now I need to have my dress made up sooner. I need something really special."

Not this again. "I hear Labrons has a good selection." Maybe they'd all be bought out and she'd have an excuse not to have to bedeck herself in a frilly outfit just to please Garrett and his sister.

Amelia joined them. "Oh, I forgot. I have to run by the library today. Do you mind if I go with Miss Beauchamps?"

"No, that's fine. But come right back. Not dilly dallying." She was even sounding like someone's mother.

"Well, come on with me then." Juliana departed, with Amelia trailing after her.

The child turned. "I'm going to bring back several books to read to the littler children tonight." She swiped a hand across her eyes as the door closed behind her.

What brought on Amelia's tears? Why would doing such a kind deed upset the girl?

She sucked in a breath beneath her ill-fitting corset, blaming no one except herself for its too-tight condition. She'd begun using the front-closing models since her mother wasn't there to assist her. How was her mother faring without Rebecca to tally the inventory, bring Mother her tea, and keep track of all the incoming and outgoing stock from the store, plus perform whatever little duties Mother sent her way? She stifled a laugh. And to think people had believed she was spoiled. Yes, she'd had anything a child could ask for and many fine belongings she'd never wished for nor needed. But she was to be an example to the community of what *could be* if only they purchased all these items from the Daggenhart's store.

Her mind wandered to the man in the rear room. What a relief that Garrett wasn't pursuing the librarian. She chewed her lower lip as she went to the back, drawn by some invisible cord that connected the two of them. Garrett looked up from the table, his dark eyes piercing hers before she could look away, pinning her there. A current chased through her and she trembled.

"I reckon you remember my brother." His hands held the wide piece of hardwood steady.

"Yes, of course." Was her new world about to get even smaller?

"He sent word he wants to stay with me tonight. Didn't think to mention it earlier."

Her breath caught in her chest. "So your brother will be at the inn, too?" Both of her rescuers there to remind her of her past.

He shrugged and averted his gaze down to the wood. "Don't know for how long, other than when he's in town. There's a cabin out by the site that Pa told him to use."

"He's out there by himself?" She took two steps closer and ran a finger over the smooth wood, sensing Garrett watching her.

She turned to face him.

"Him and his rifle." Although he gave her a half smile, the twitch near his left eye made her think he, too, had some concerns.

She'd considered purchasing a small pistol for herself. *Just in case.* With Myron due out of prison soon, she prayed he'd stay far away. As she pushed a stray lock of hair from her temple, one of her hairpins fell, and Garrett quickly caught it in his free broad hand. He held it out to her and she took it, her fingers brushing against the warmth of his. Her heart rate sped up.

"I think I know what color this oak will be with the varnish on it." He moved one step closer to the table.

"Oh?" Her breath caught. She really had to loosen this corset. Either that or stop eating the fluffy biscuits Jo Christy baked for the inn.

He reached toward her, and when his rough fingers grazed her jaw and jostled her fallen curl she immediately stepped away, reliving the moment when Myron had grabbed her neck and wrapped a rope around it. She pressed her hand to her throat.

Garrett's eyes widened. "I'm sorry." He ran a finger along his own square jaw line and then pointed to hers. "Just meant to say that with the varnish, the wood should be the same pretty golden-brown color as your hair. Didn't mean to upset you."

Pretty color? Gone were the golden tresses she'd sported as a girl. She'd welcomed the drab brown locks that replaced her blonde curls.

"Miss Daggenhart?"

"Yes?" She shook her head. "I told you not to call me that."

"Janie, please…" He held up his hands.

She backed away. "I'm Rebecca Hart now, not Janie Daggenhart, and you need to remember that."

Her words came out brusquer than she'd intended, and his features flashed in hurt before settling into a mask. "It just slipped out. Why call yourself Rebecca?"

"That's my first name."

"Truly?"

"Yes." She tried to stuff the stray curl into the rest of the mass with another pin but struggled to secure it without a mirror to guide her.

"I hope you know I'd never hurt you. I'd never harm any woman." He cleared his throat. "And as long as you're under my protection, I swear no man will ever hurt you again."

A strange chill went through her. Under his protection? She rubbed her hand against her throat. "Did my father send you here? Was this woodworking job just a ruse?"

"A ruse?" His dark eyebrows pulled together. "What's that mean?"

"I mean are you really here to watch over me? Taking the job was just a trick?"

"Maybe the first part of what you said, but not a trick. And not the Father you think." Garrett stared at her, his lips slightly parted. Then he closed his eyes tightly.

Was he praying?

०३४०

Moose plunked down in the overstuffed chair next to the couch in the inn's main salon as Garrett set his newspaper down. Although there were several area newspaper publishers in the bustling town, Cordelia subscribed to the original paper, which had the most subscribers.

Moose swiped at the paper. "See any ads for a tall, dark, handsome lumberjack to sweep some gal off her feet?"

"Heard you already met the librarian."

"Yup. Ain't she a purty little thing?"

"If you go for the crow look, I guess."

"She don't look like no crow." Moose scowled at him and raised a fist but dropped it when Garrett glared back.

"Dressed in those mourning clothes she does."

"She ain't in mourning." Moose bobbed his head, as though agreeing with himself. "I asked."

Garrett sighed. He hated it when his anger flared, but his little brother had a way of getting under his skin right quick. "Why's she dressed in black then?"

"Makes her feel more…hmmm, some word that means powerful, awthora-something, she said." Moose laughed. "Authoritative—sounds like a book writer. Anyways, she's gotta look serious for her patrons."

"Her patrons?"

"Yup. All the folks traipsing in and out of that library building of hers."

Such as the orphan girl. "Hey, brother, I need to tell you something." Just in case his brother recognized the girl they'd rescued.

"Ain't you always tellin' me something?" Moose extended a hand as though to slap Garrett playfully on the side of the head, but he stayed him by grabbing his wrist.

"Stop. You act like you're twelve years old sometimes." Garrett scowled at him. "Do you remember Miss Daggenhart?"

Moose dropped the newspaper onto his lap, his features softening, reminding Garrett of the young boy who'd been with him that night. "How could I forget? Is she all right? Pa said that fella who hurt her is out of jail."

His heart clutched in his chest. "*He's out?* And when were you gonna tell me that?"

"Just did. Sorry."

Garrett squeezed his hands into fists. "She's here."

"What?" Moose cocked his head.

"Janie's here. In this town. In this very establishment, right now." He'd seen her skirts swaying as she'd gone upstairs fifteen minutes earlier clutching the bannister he'd installed the previous week.

"I'll be a two-legged race horse." His brother's jaw slackened.

"I'm working at her store." Garrett reached for his coffee cup, resting on the table he'd built for the inn, grabbed it, and threw back a swig of the strong brew.

"What?"

"She's got a mercantile across from the train docks."

Moose swiped a hand through his hair. "What kind of dumb Pa..."

"Sh! You're too loud, someone might hear you, but I was thinking the same thing. What kind of father lets his daughter come up here by herself?" He heard footsteps descending the hall stairs.

"Miss Beauchamps says they have very little crime here and the sheriff is top rate."

"I'd like to meet him."

Moose emitted a low whistle. "Yeah, I had a long talk with him earlier today."

"About what?"

"Someone is camping out in an old shack not far from the new logging site."

"One of the former lumberjacks?" Oftentimes someone injured would remain behind until he recovered.

"I don't know. Can't ever catch him there, but it gives me the willies. I've got Pa's shotgun and all my hatchets and the like, but I can't hardly sleep out there. I can tell you, 'cause you're my brother, but I told the sheriff I was fine." Moose stretched, expanding his chest. "After all, doesn't everyone think a big man like me can handle anything?"

Garrett shook his head. "That would be a mistake, thinking you could."

"So you won't tease that I'm acting like a little girl if I stay at the inn?"

"No. I'd never mistake you for a female. Especially not with that beard."

"Speaking of which, where is yours, pretty boy?"

Heavy footsteps carried down the hall as someone approached from the rear of the inn. A strongly built man, with salt-and-pepper hair beneath a thick wool cap, stood in the archway. "Mr. Christy?"

Moose stood. "Yes, Sheriff Edwards, and this is my brother."

Garrett stood and extended a hand, feeling his knees wobble slightly as the man delivered a bone-crunching grasp, one even stronger than he, Moose, or their father performed, and that was saying something. "Garrett Christy—nice to meet you, Sheriff." He resisted the urge to rub his hand after the man released his aching fingers.

"We've confirmed one of the loggers was indeed injured and left to recuperate. A Mr. Giles. He's got a squaw who's supposed to be tending him out there."

Garrett cringed inside at the man's derogatory term. For Misty Fawn's sake, and her children, he longed to correct the man's attitude. Instead, he tamped down the steam building in him.

Moose frowned. "No sign of her. Looks like a single man is staying there."

"Might be she left him. Or went back to her tribe if they needed her there. That happens." The sheriff's pleasant tone of voice reflected no bigotry.

Garrett relaxed his shoulders. Who knew, maybe the lawman, like many people from this area, might be Chippewa himself.

"That logger, Giles, had permission from the former owner to stay. They weren't expecting you fellas till spring."

"Right."

Sheriff Edwards frowned. "And why are you here early?"

"I'm supposed to survey each structure, which I've already done. I'll be going back out on the new train line tomorrow." Moose grinned. "Sure am looking forward to that, sheriff, instead of having to tramp to the camp."

A smile tugged at the man's lips before he directed his attention to Garrett. "What about you?"

"I'm making shelving for Miss Dag...Miss Hart's mercantile." And falling deeper into her hazel eyes every time she looked at him.

Heels clicked against the wood floor, crossing the short distance between the parlor and the main salon. Rebecca's pink nose matched her lace scarf, the only decorative and colorful item on her person. "And he's doing a beautiful job, Sheriff. Achoo!" Rebecca took a step back from the entryway.

Behind her, Cordelia descended the staircase. "Bless you, dear," she called down.

Rebecca retrieved a flimsy looking excuse for a handkerchief, from her pocket, and pressed it to her nose.

When Cordelia reached her, she placed her hand on Rebecca's forehead. "Not you, too?" Then she took Rebecca by her shoulders, turned her to the stairs, and pointed upward. "We'll bring a tray up for you. Don't fret."

Chapter Seven

Broken ice along the Lake Michigan and Lake Huron shorelines released frigid damp air permeating Garrett's wool clothing as he strode up the walkway to the store. Rebecca lay abed at the inn, battling a spring cold. He hoped what ailed her wasn't caused by all the sawdust he'd kicked up in the shop. Regardless, she'd given him the key and he'd made his way down State Street to the mercantile. He ducked into the muddy alley between the store and the tobacconist and stopped. Maybe he should have gone through the front door, but it didn't seem right. So he continued down the dim alleyway, hoping the boot scraper out back could remove the muck from his boot bottoms.

Rounding the corner, he spied a wad of half-burnt pipe tobacco dumped out on an overturned box that leaned against the building. *Darned fool.* If that had any spark left in it and the wooden crate had caught fire, the building could have gone up in flames. Who had put that there? He scowled at the space behind the businesses on that block. Mr. Chambers, the gun shop owner on the other side of the building, often took his pipe out back while his wife waited on his customers. If Garrett didn't have so much work to complete, he'd seek out the man and tell him to stay far away from Rebecca's building when he smoked.

Garrett stomped to the back door, too steamed to pay attention to something niggling at him. He paused on the stoop before swiveling to look back. His own big boot tracks covered most of the footprints someone else had left. They'd been smaller than his, but that wasn't unusual. And they were narrower, which also wasn't a surprise. But the prints seemed larger than those left by Rebecca's boots...but maybe. With word that Peevey was out, his nerves were on edge.

He located the low, steel boot scraper to the left of the door and scraped off as much mud as he could. Turning, he narrowed his eyes at the brown remnants on the box. Might that clump be tealeaves and not tobacco? Rebecca took a notion that the remnants from her tea ball should be emptied out on the struggling daffodils—said the tannic acid in it helped them flourish. He'd wanted to tell her his ma always threw down old fish with her bulbs in the fall, when she'd replanted them, but thought he should pick his battles. If she wanted to toss tealeaves outside her own store, so be it. But why throw them atop a crate?

He inserted the key into the lock and groaned when it didn't immediately open. As he fiddled with it, the lock cylinder produced grating noises, as though already loose. He'd try to speak with the locksmith later, but his good intentions wouldn't make that happen. Between working at the inn and for Rebecca, his list of things to do was lengthening and the time to do them in shortening. At least Rebecca hadn't mentioned any problems with the entry door lock, so if this failed, he'd go around to the front. The mechanism finally gave, and he opened the door and went inside, carefully scanning the room for signs of an intruder. *Nothing.* All his tools right where he'd left him. He exhaled. Those carving implements had cost him a pretty penny, but they remained nestled in their flannel wrap.

Whistling, he set up his workplace. Then he walked to the front of the store. All looked in order. He pulled back the curtains from the window and unlocked and checked the door. Perfectly smooth, opening and closing. The locksmith was an elderly man who'd been in his line of work for decades. He'd installed the inn's locks, but had been ill recently and needed to finish putting in the door locksets on the top floor. The third level held no occupants, though, and likely wouldn't until summer and the tourists arrived.

Garrett returned to his workbench and began sanding down a cabriole table leg. The curving wood reminded him of a woman's figure and he paused momentarily in his motions. He'd designed the piece. Was his distraction by Rebecca and her womanliness affecting his work? If so, she'd not complained about all he'd produced so far. *Still.* He swallowed as he set aside his sandpaper.

The doorbell jingled. Already? Had Rebecca pushed herself to come in after he'd urged her to stay put at the inn? But when he rose and went through the privacy curtain to the front of the store, he found Jo and Tom waiting. And kissing. He rolled his eyes heavenward.

Although his father described his eldest son as a "man of strong emotions," Garrett had managed to constrain most of his romantic feelings until recently, when he'd seen Janie, or rather Rebecca, again. Ma always scolded that he should withhold any grand displays of affection until he'd found the woman he'd marry—sure that passionate nature would get him into trouble. Thankfully, it hadn't. Although after her death he'd indulged in some activities he knew she'd rue, but he'd always ceased his kissing the tavern girls before things escalated and before they'd asked for money to continue their "attentions". After seeing what that weasel Peevey had done to Rebecca, Garrett could only wonder what she must think about men who "paid her any mind," as his Ma used to say. Though Myron Peevey shouldn't be compared to other men. Peevey's father was one of the worst abusive drunks around, but so were many other men of the woods and that didn't make their sons become deranged. Right from the beginning, before Mr. Peevey lost his wife and started his decline, Myron had something strange about him. And it wasn't just the way he trailed Janie Daggenhart like a puppy. Not that anyone dared allow their pets loose in town—for those small animals were often found dead, near the river. Garrett shivered. Peevey had been a killer from the beginning, yet he kept that aspect of himself hidden, just as he made a display of his dedication to Janie. And that betrayal had to have affected her and made Rebecca Hart who she was today—a woman unlikely to accept the type of affection Tom displayed toward Jo.

Garrett groaned. "Hey, you two, you're in a public place."

"Pooh, this isn't public—it's just you." Jo laughed and kissed Tom again.

Tom Jeffries pulled Jo close and pressed his lips to her forehead. "I've never been so happy in all my life."

"Me, too." Jo's satisfied sigh grated on Garrett's taut nerves, but he couldn't say why.

You're jealous.

Am not. So now he was arguing with himself. Or was that I Am speaking to him?

The two kissed again. Garrett's cheeks heated. Couldn't deny he wanted to enjoy such happiness with someone he loved. How would it be to kiss Rebecca and have her glow like his sister did?

"We're trying to plan our wedding." Tom arched an eyebrow.

Jo nibbled her lower lip. "But we're running into trouble with scheduling because of the Lumberjacks' Ball."

"Yeah, I've heard about it." Had no intention of going.

Jo strode toward him, her hand outstretched, clutching an envelope, its seal broken. "Pa sent us all a letter."

Garrett took it and scanned the missive. "Pa's gonna give up lumberjacking? I don't believe it."

Tom joined them. "We need to let Moose know what your Pa thinks. And I'm concerned about my own job, too. No camp—no students, unless I'm hired here or in one of the other small towns closer to the camp."

His future brother-in-law needed that job. Garrett rubbed his jaw. "Moose is young."

"But he's capable." Jo's lower lip protruded as it did when she was about to be stubborn.

He wasn't pursuing this conversation, because as far as he was concerned their younger brother was a man of action and not one for thoughtful planning, which was required to manage a camp. What would happen to all their lumber camp friends if Pa followed through?

◌◈◌

The door to Rebecca's bedchamber drifted open. Amelia stood there, holding Sister Mary Lou's hand and clutching a pitiful-looking first daffodil, its fledgling petals almost transparent.

The girl broke free and ran to the bed. "You can't be sick, Miss Hart! I don't want you to die."

"Oh, hush, now." Sister Mary Lou's dark skirts swished as she approached the bed, bringing the chill of the outdoor air with her, and a faint hint of incense.

Rebecca pushed up on her elbows. "I've just got a spring cold. I'm not dying."

She brushed a lock of the girl's hair back from her eyes. What would it be like to have a child? To pull her own daughter into an embrace?

Amelia dropped the flower on the bed, threw her arms around Rebecca, and wept. Startled, Rebecca froze. The small hands were tight against the back of her neck, evoking memories of the moment the rope had pulled tight and began to hoist her up. But this touch was a loving one and slowly the chill she'd experienced ebbed away, replaced by the warmth of tiny fingers tugging at her bed-strewn hair.

"Will you look at all her pretty hair, Sister Mary Lou?" Amelia sat on the bed and began to arrange Rebecca's waist-length locks around her shoulders. "Can I brush it?"

Before she could answer, the child had crossed the wood floor and retrieved her boar's head brush, its silver-plated and embossed handle in need of a good polishing.

The nun leaned in and whispered, "I tried to keep her back at the orphanage, but she'd become almost hysterical. She believed you were dying."

Soon, little Amelia had brushed all the tangles from Rebecca's tresses. She returned the brush to the dresser and brought the ornate, hand-held mirror back. "Look."

Rebecca's hand shook as she held the reflecting glass aloft. Sister Mary Lou pulled the heavy drapes back from the windows, allowing in more light.

Hazel eyes gazed back at her. Twin swirls of pink glowed on her high cheekbones. She held the mirror further away. Dark curls framed her face and a decade seemed to have fallen away from her complexion, making her look closer to her twenty-seven years than the woman of middling years she'd appeared lately. She looked almost pretty.

Heavy footfalls sounded in the hallway outside the room and the door swung in. "Are you all right?"

Rebecca looked up to see Garrett Christy, his cheeks flushed, wringing his hat with his beefy hands. Right behind him, the priest appeared and gently pushed the gaping lumberjack aside. Rebecca pulled her bedcovers up to her chin.

"Miss Hart, the children from the orphanage came to me." The priest glanced at Sister Mary Lou, who appeared to be rolling her eyes skyward. "They thought you were dead."

"Do I look dead, Father?" Rebecca laughed as Amelia hid behind Sister Mary Lou.

"She sure don't." Garrett's Adam's apple bobbed. "You look pretty as a peach with your hair like that."

The priest cast a stern look in the other man's direction before returning his attention to Rebecca, who shrank further beneath her Ivory soap-scented covers.

Sister Mary Lou wrapped an arm around Amelia and brought her forward. "I'm afraid the other girls took Amy's alarm over Miss Hart's illness a little too far and came up with their own dire conjectures."

Garrett frowned as though he was trying to understand the nun's words. "Do ya mean like that silly game about those new-fangled telephones and taking messages that get all mixed up?"

St. Ignace boasted their own telephone exchange, available to those who could afford the service. But when Rebecca had visited Burt's Bank, where the switchboard was located, and inquired about the fee, she knew her father wouldn't agree to a store phone until she began to produce a hefty profit margin.

"The *Grapevine* game," Amelia called out. "And that's been played since before Mr. Bell invented telephones."

Sister Mary Lou drew in a deep breath. "Regardless, as we can all see, Miss Hart simply has a cold and is in no mortal danger."

She might be in no mortal danger, but from the gleam in Garrett's eyes, Rebecca found herself in a new sort of danger. One she didn't care to face.

���

After saying their goodbyes, Garrett left Rebecca's room and the inn and returned to the shop. Deep in his thoughts of how pretty she'd looked, he soon found himself walking ahead of Amy and Sister Mary Lou. The duo trotted after him.

A train whistle drew his attention momentarily toward the tracks, across the street, and beyond to the Straits of Mackinac. Across that sapphire water lay the Christy lumber camp, nestled in the woods. Hard to believe that instead of hefting an ax or working one end of a saw he'd be creating something beautiful from the lumber culled from the forests.

As he easily unlocked the mercantile front door, he vowed to talk with the locksmith and to keep watch for any other indications that someone had been smoking behind their building.

He turned to the child. "Amy, have you or Miss Hart been tossing spent tealeaves out back behind the shop?"

"Yes. In that little area where I got a blossom for her. I think it is helping."

The nun, standing behind the girl, rolled her eyes again, and Garrett almost laughed.

After waiting for Sister Mary Lou and Amy to enter the store, Garrett followed them in, the scent of freshly sawn wood an intoxicant to him. He missed the piney woods. Missed his father and friends. But God had called him to come out and begin using his gifts of crafting furniture.

"What's this?" Amy pointed to the ornate bookcase he'd just finished.

Although he'd intended to sell that piece elsewhere, Rebecca liked it so much she'd purchased it for the store. She understood that he would be making other copies if commissioned to do so. Already someone had left their name with Rebecca while he'd been in the back working on the new armoire that would hold soft goods such as yarn and fabric. She'd asked for casters on the bottom, in case she wanted to move the furniture around more easily. Only a woman would think of such a silly thing. Much safer and sturdier to simply build-in your displays where you wished them to remain.

"That's Miss Hart's new bookcase for all the maps, books, and paper goods she plans to sell." If they ever arrived. At this rate, summer season would be here and gone and the store not yet fully stocked.

Sister Mary Lou smiled and lifted a wooden cube that he'd outfitted with an "X" shaped divider in the middle. "And this?"

"I thought that might work to hold stationary and cards."

The nun's smile faded. "I hate to say this, but with all of the new businesses in the area, Miss Hart will face stiff competition. A new bookstore and a stationers have both opened further down State Street."

Nearer the more popular shopping area. Trusting in You, God, and praying Rebecca does, too.

Chapter Eight

Rebecca stripped away April's calendar sheet, saving it for the tinder pile. Her first month had ended and her father had yet to return. Her helpers consisted of a pint-sized orphan, a nun whose sales could help get her out of debt, and a lumberjack handyman who reminded her every day of her past and whose presence had her reconsidering her future.

April had been a busy month, which had included a surprisingly vibrant Easter spent with Garrett's family. Poor Miss Beauchamps, who'd not been included even though Richard expressed a fondness for her as well as his opinion that a well-educated woman who was several years older than him could not possibly be interested in a lumberjack. And Rebecca hadn't corrected his misconception. Perhaps she should have. But she had her own romantic dilemma, for her appreciation of Garrett Christy grew stronger every day.

He joined her in the front, carrying two mugs full of coffee. "Here you go. Thought you might enjoy a break."

"Thank you." Taking a sip, she appreciated that he'd added enough cream to make it just the way she liked.

"I added sugar—two lumps." Tiny lines crinkled around his dark eyes.

What would it be like to look into those chocolate brown eyes every night? "Perfectly prepared."

"May already. Hard to believe." His eyebrows pulled together as he swiped the sheet from the counter and held it aloft.

"You've accomplished so much." Not one corner was untouched by his expertise—from the built-in armoires, to the shelving, to the cubes for dry goods, and to the new counter space.

"Thank you kindly, but I'm thinkin' you're running out of work for me."

She almost dropped her coffee and he reached out to steady her hand, sending a spark through her.

"Listen, I've been wanting to talk with you about something." This close, she could smell his spicy aftershave mingling with the scent of cedar and pine from his woodwork.

Her heart pounded.

"Actually, I have a couple of things I'd like to say. One is that if you'd really like to go to that Lumberjacks' Ball then maybe I could practice the dances."

"Uh…" Her mouth opened, but she couldn't finish her sentence. Why had she been expecting him to make a profession of admiration for her? Her cheeks heated. But wasn't this invitation saying he found her worthy of escorting? Yet, if she were to be a successful businesswoman how could she be consorting with her hired help? That wouldn't bode well for her.

"You don't have to tell me right now." The smile tugging at his lips vanished.

She ran her tongue over her dry lips. "What was the other thing?"

Garrett exhaled loudly, took a long swig of his coffee, and then took the obsolete calendar sheet to the tinderbox. "I have to find more work, ongoing jobs, for me to stay here and not return to the lumber camp."

"But this is a boom town. Surely you'll have no difficulty."

He shoved a hand through his hair. "Lots of workers have flocked to the area, and many folks are willing to settle for basics. The wealthy summer residents haven't yet returned."

"Have you gotten commissions from your work here?"

"Yes, a few, but not enough to support me and…" He took another drink of his black coffee.

"Do you have any ideas?" Several ran through her mind. *Marry me and help run the store.* She dismissed that notion outright. "What about remaining at the inn?"

He shook his head, causing an ebony lock of hair to fall across his pale forehead. "I'll keep looking, but I don't think I can wait until June when more of the wealthy vacationers return."

"I'll keep my ears open and ask, too. And I'll put an advertisement in all four newspapers." She had to do something.

Suddenly, the excitement of opening a new store loomed pointless without Garrett there beside her.

०३४०

Three glorious weeks of May arrived with walks in the park, meals shared at the inn, games of checkers and all manner of card games, and the welcome addition of laughter back into Rebecca's life. Life truly was beginning anew. As was their new custom, she and Garrett took their morning break together, over coffee, accompanied by one of Jo's new creations from the bakery. This morning she'd created a vanilla streusel breakfast muffin with a dollop of cream cheese in the center.

After sinking her teeth into the pastry, Rebecca savored the taste. "Mmm, this is delicious."

Garrett nibbled at his and set it back down on its plate. *How unlike him.* He wrapped both of his hands around his coffee mug and took a long drink. All morning long he'd been pacing in the back, in between applying coats of varnish to a cabinet door.

He cleared his throat. "I've got a lead on Mackinac Island for a fine craftsman position."

"Oh?"

"You know I've had no offers here and we're bumping up on June soon."

She swallowed hard. "What do you know about this job?"

"I'm going over tomorrow to find out. I have an interview."

"Tomorrow?" Her voice squeaked like one of the mice she'd chased out that morning. He was leaving her?

"Yes, and I have permission from Sister Mary Lou to take Amy with me."

Startled at this statement, her hands rocked her mug almost spilling the contents. "Amelia will go, too?"

"Yes, she has two brothers and a sister at the orphanage on Mackinac Island." He took another long draught of his coffee.

"What?" Her voice came out between a shriek of outrage and astonishment. "They sent that child over here by herself when she has family still there?"

The corner of his mouth twitched. "My feelings exactly, and I intend to follow up on that."

Exhaling loudly, Rebecca went to her work chair and sat, motioning for Garrett to join her. "I'm shocked. I had no idea." Which showed how little she knew about the sweet child. And the same feelings expressed her reaction to Garrett going away.

"She talks to Jo, so don't be thinkin' it's anything special I did." He raised his eyebrows apologetically as he slid into the seat across from her. He leaned forward, setting his elbows on his knees as he clasped his cup. He looked so longingly at her that she had to avert her gaze.

"Ah, when she gets her cupcakes and cookies I bet." She stared down at her coffee mug, clutched in her lap.

"Yup."

Each evening, after dinner, any baked goods threatening to go stale were sent to the orphanage. Amelia had been the child sent to get them, walking back from the inn with Garrett.

"Anyway, I'm bringing her and…" He bent his head and she met his dark eyes. "I want to find a home where all those kids can stay together."

"Really?" Her heart warmed. "I've been praying that Amelia could be placed in a good home." Like with her. But now…three siblings…that was too much for a single woman to manage.

"Would you agree to pray with me that my trip will be successful tomorrow?"

Flabbergasted, all she could manage was to nod. Although he seemed like a believer, and attended church, Garrett didn't discuss his faith much—rather, he lived it.

"You know…" Two red spots formed on his cheeks. He had such a handsome face, how could he not have married by now? "One of the last times I petitioned God as hard as I've been praying about this, *He used me* to save the prettiest girl in the county from drowning."

"What?" Suddenly light-headed, she set her coffee mug down and Garrett did the same.

He took her hands in his, rubbing his thumb over her knuckles and sending a chill through her. "Long ago, I prayed all one week that you'd pay some attention to me when I went into town to your store. Peevey had been gone so long, I'd hoped you'd forgotten him and how he trailed after you like a lost pup. I came to the store and asked your pa if you could attend the dance with me. They had a Lumberjacks' Ball out near our camp. Your pa laughed at me. *Laughed.* And he said to ask you."

She stiffened. "Why didn't you?"

He raised both eyebrows. "I did and you ignored me."

"No, you didn't!"

"I did. And I can even tell you when."

"What?" She shook her head. "Garrett Christy, don't start telling tales now."

"It's true for certain." He motioned to the ladder leaning against the wall, so Rebecca and her future shop help could reach the top shelves. "You were at the top shelf of your pa's store, dusting with some feather thing."

She nodded. "Yes, I did use a feather duster, but you never asked me to any dance."

"Yes ma'am, I did, even though I couldn't dance a lick." His voice took on the gravelly tones as it did when he was younger.

"What did you ask me?"

"I said, 'Will you go with me to the Lumberjacks' Ball?' And you looked at me like I'd lost my mind."

She frowned, trying to recollect.

"Then you pointed to the door, as though I should leave."

"I do remember once, that horrible week, you coming in and asking for…baseballs I think it was."

"Baseballs?"

"Oh my goodness! Your Kentucky accent was so much thicker back then. It sounded like you were asking for balls for the lumberjacks! Not a Lumberjacks' Ball. Not a dance. My father told me there was a new baseball team and he'd stocked up—the new baseballs were by the door. So, I pointed them out to you."

He chuckled. "And here all this time I'd thought you'd given me the boot out the door." His face began to transform, and the yearning in his eyes matched that in her heart.

Chapter Nine

S unlight sparkled off deep blue waves as the boat carrying Garrett and Amy crossed halfway through the straits to Mackinac Island, positioned between the Upper and Lower Peninsulas. Temperatures hovered near fifty degrees, bringing providential warmth this day. He felt genuinely blessed, in his heart, for the first time in years. Yet, he had no reason to feel so fortunate if he looked at the "facts." Fact was he was a single lumberjack who no longer wanted to be part of the lumbering business, but he couldn't allow his younger brother to take on management of a new camp. Also, fact was he wanted to court Rebecca, if he could only get past her prickly defenses. But he'd find a way.

Garrett. That same voice whispered to him, but it wasn't Amy—who was gazing out over the bow. Two days earlier, he'd been sure he'd heard someone wake him in the night and tell him to take the child to the island with him. Of course, he'd not shared that little bit with Sister Mary Lou, lest she refer him to a mental asylum.

After removing his wool cap, he shoved a hand back through his hair and then stuffed the hat into his pocket.

The little girl looked up with wide blue eyes. "Do you think they'll remember me?"

Despite the seriousness of her expression, he had to chuckle. "Hasn't been quite a year, already, has it?

She frowned and her lower lip wobbled. "Jimmy was only a baby, and now he'll be almost two."

"Two?" Something jabbed his chest like a sharp pang. Was the sensation compassion—something he'd almost thought he'd lost in the camps? Not necessarily from the people but from always spending his energy watching over his sister, to protect her.

The girl's ringlets bobbed up and down as she nodded. "I'm going to squeeze the stuffing out of him."

"Better not!" He laughed. "We'll stop at Doud's Market and pick him up a treat—a toy or something."

"He'd like that." Her dimple disappeared. "But I don't really know, since I haven't seen him in so long."

"You've really missed him, haven't you?"

"Uh huh."

"I miss my old friend, Sven." The Swede had been his closest friend for years.

"Will you see him again?"

"Yep. He'll be marrying Ruth and bringin' her three little sisters up to the new lumber camp." And Garrett missed the days he'd spent card playing with friends and the antics of the passel of kids who'd always made him smile. He might not be as educated as his future brother-in-law nor have little ones follow him like Pied Piper, but children often took a liking to Garrett for some reason.

Pa always said it was because he was generous with them—bringing them little treats from the mercantile if their mothers were sick. Or accompanying his own ma on occasion to tote pies, cakes, and the like around when there was a birthday to celebrate. And he'd always have some small, wood-carved object for the celebrated child. What would it be like to have a family of his own?

As they rounded the back curve of the island and made the turn, he pointed ahead. "See that big building up there on the cliff?"

Amy narrowed her eyes and raised a hand to shield them from the sun and wind. "The Grand Hotel? I watched it being built. My parents owned a shop right near there."

When she rested her hand on the railing, he covered her gloved hand with his. Warmth stirred within him. He could have a ready-made family of four, if only Rebecca had understood him and accepted his invitation to the Woodsmen's Ball a decade earlier. If he'd not, instead, ended up fishing that night. If she'd gone, would Peevey have tried to kill her another night? *Likely so.*

You were where you needed to be.

Amy's lips didn't move, but a voice had spoken to his heart and chills coursed through him as the boat sliced through the water toward the island. A horn blast announced their approach, and Amy almost jumped out of the new shoes Rebecca had given her. He pressed a hand to the child's shoulder to steady her.

All these years he'd been disappointed, becoming distant with God, because of how things had turned out. After the trial, Mr. Daggenhart had refused to allow Garrett to speak with Rebecca. He had another opportunity now, but this orphan—what did she have?

God, why did you allow this to happen?

Seemed strange to be talking to God so familiarly after so much time. Yes, he'd attended services when the stump preacher came out to the camp, but half the time he'd been stewing over Peevey's light prison sentence. A niggling began in the back of his mind. Would Tom and Jo really keep an eye on Rebecca today while he was gone? He'd have to trust they would. Them and God.

He smiled. The Easter service had been special to him. Since then, it felt like an old friend had come back into his life—much like finding Rebecca again after all these years.

As they docked, Garrett kept ahold of the little girl's hand as she bobbed up and down on her tiptoes. It was a habit he, too, had when he got agitated over something. Someday, his own children might display the same behavior.

Soon they'd disembarked and made their way down the wharf to the island's main street. From the fort above, cannon fire marked the hour. Almost ten. They'd need to get their business done quickly, because the ferry was operating on a short day with the off-season. Many islanders lived in St. Ignace during the winter months. It looked as if quite a few people were returning early and waited at the dock for their baggage.

Unencumbered, Garrett and Amy set off for the church and the orphanage. He eyed the bike rental stands.

"Do you know how to ride a bicycle, Amy?"

"Yessir." She gave him a look like Jo did when she thought he'd asked something daft. "Can you ride?" She glanced at the double-seaters, longing etched on her tiny face.

"Afraid not, sunshine." He resisted the sudden urge to push the child's hair from her eyes. Ma always called Jo "sunshine" and so had Pa when she was little. He missed his Ma something fierce, and if he was honest with himself, he had a strong hankering to spend time with Pa.

"What you looking at?"

"Oh, just over to Mackinaw City, where my Pa is." And the camp and his old friends.

"If my pa was still alive, I'd hop on the next boat over and go see him." With that, the child turned on her boot heel, pulled free from his grasp, and strode up the boardwalk toward Doud's Market. Apparently being on the island brought out the imp in Amy.

When she turned to glance back at him, her flushed face was tear-streaked. He shoved his hands in his pockets and wove through the shoppers on the sidewalk. Luckily there were few people between him and Amy and he spied her as she ducked into the mercantile.

A Chippewa woman, who reminded him of Misty Fawn's mother, sat in the sheltered alcove outside a dried goods store. She displayed a beaded turtle and named a price he couldn't resist. He gave her the coins and resumed his chase after Amy. Her toddler brother, Jimmy, couldn't have this toy, but Amy might enjoy the reminder after she returned to St. Ignace. The island was named after Gitchee Manitou, the Great Turtle, and was the spiritual home of the Ojibway. The Native people could call the Lord what they wanted, as far as he was concerned, for there was only one God amongst all.

Once inside Doud's Market, he scanned the aisles. The wood planked floors bore witness to the recent damp weather, with wet footprints marring them. Amy popped out from a cubby and pressed a soft cotton elephant into his hands and a slingshot. "For Jimmy and Russell."

He held the latter item aloft. "Do you really think they'll let your brother have this?"

She chewed her lower lip and then snatched it from his hands. Soon she returned with a cloth bag full of marbles and a wooden Indian maiden doll, attired in a brown fringed gown. "Russ likes these and I got something for Regina, too."

"Good choices." He took the item then playfully mussed her hair.

"I think my little sister is old enough for a doll like this now. She can dress her up if she wants. And I bet Miss Hart would let me have some scraps from the ends of bolts to make some doll clothes with."

"Sure."

She looked up with bright eyes. "Are you going to marry Miss Hart?"

"I…" His mouth dropped open, but he closed it and swallowed hard. "Lord willing."

"Lord willing…I don't think I've heard that saying before."

He laughed. "Where I grew up they'd say, Lord willing and if the creek don't rise." But the creek between them may have risen too high to ever have a true courtship, much less a wedding.

"Doesn't rise." She arched an eyebrow at him like a miniature adult.

"It's an expression, Amy." He drew in a deep breath and then exhaled slowly. "Means you're hoping and praying for something, but it's all up to God."

"Like me and my brothers and sister getting a new family?"

"Right."

A clerk walked up the aisle to them. "May I be of assistance?"

"Think we've got what we need."

"Fine, the register is right there around the corner."

"I think he wants you to pay right now," Amy whispered.

Garrett cupped his hand around his mouth and whispered into her ear, "I think you're right."

She giggled as they approached the dour-faced man at the register and paid.

Outside the store, a cab pulled up to the curb. "Need a ride, mister?" the driver called out.

Amy shook her head emphatically. "Not from you, Mr. Stan, you drive too fast!"

The young man lifted his navy cap brim. "That you, Miss Amelia?"

"Yes, it is."

He whistled. "Look at how grown up you're getting."

She bobbed a curtsey and drew out her skirt, displaying an excess of fabric that Garrett rarely had seen. Jo and Ma said all that extra cloth was for rich folks and unnecessary.

"My new ma had this made for me." Pink flushed the child's cheeks.

Her new ma?

"Sure is good to see you. That your new pa?"

She grabbed Garrett's hand. "Sure is."

Garrett's mouth dropped open.

"Well, if that ain't something." The driver tugged at his hat and slapped the reins, moving his carriage on.

Garrett gave Amy what he hoped was a very stern look. He was no parent and he had no experience in correcting children, but *a lie was a lie.*

"I'm sorry, Mr. Christy, but something rose up inside me and I had to say that because…because…" Through her tears, she looked up at him with an intense longing that he recognized—a yearning for something that might never be. She wanted Rebecca and him to marry and then take in her and her siblings.

In an instant, she turned, crossed the alleyway, and ran up the boardwalk past the park. No one ever said this would be easy. *Lord, I came here for the job at the Grand Hotel, not to find myself a family.*

An hour later, after meeting with the priest and the nun who served as administrators of the orphanage, Garrett said his goodbyes to Amy and her siblings and departed for his interview at the Grand Hotel.

The craftsmen's supervisor, Mr. Belongia, met him in the lobby and then escorted Garrett throughout the beautiful hotel. "We need the rooms to be as well-appointed on the inside as our exterior suggests it should be—and it isn't right now."

"I understand." Garrett proceeded to point out several easy embellishments that would give the men's smoking room a feeling of grandeur, combined with privacy.

They continued on, with Mr. Belongia stopping into almost every room, which required a great deal of time. Garrett tried not to check his pocket watch and thankfully there were clocks in several of the public rooms. The supervisor posed a half dozen scenarios to him, as to how Garrett would approach complicated cabinetry making tasks. They stopped in a work room, and he explained an intricate joinery procedure.

"Follow me out to the street and I'll show you where the workers lodge."

They walked down the long corridor, careful to avoid the maids and their carts as they cleaned rooms. A fresh breeze met them as they exited the building through a side door. He pointed to a cedar-sided, four story, boxy building.

Garrett stiffened. "The dormitory there?"

Mr. Belongia laughed. "No, that's for our service workers. I was pointing to that row of cottages beyond—that's for our master craftsmen. Single men are allowed a two bedroom bungalow and may have family guests. Married men have the three bedroom ones."

His own little house where he and Rebecca could live. If she'd marry him and come to the island. *That's a tall order, God, but I'm counting on you.*

"Thank you, sir, for showing me."

The supervisor turned and pointed back to the service entrance. They walked back in, Mr. Belongia explaining his plans for the next five years' projects.

Dodging the cleaning carts again, they weaved their way up the hall and into a small office with several wing chairs and took a seat.

"Well, I believe we can offer you a competitive wage, Mr. Christy." Belongia named the amount and Garrett swallowed.

He couldn't manage to speak. That was triple his lumberjack wages even in the best season.

"Of course, because of your knowledge, we'd also give you an advance."

"That's generous."

Belongia laughed. "We can keep a fellow like you busy for years if you're willing."

After they spoke for a few more minutes about the initial projects, Garrett exited the huge hotel, grinning. *I'm blessed, Lord, and the offer staggers me, but Rebecca lives in St. Ignace.*

Stepping out into the sunlight, Garrett succumbed to temptation and hired himself a cab back to the orphanage. He'd take little Amy down to the wharf, for departure, in style. *God, thank You.* But what about Rebecca? He'd give her his notice, but he'd already completed the jobs she needed done.

As the carriage approached the grey stone orphanage, it slowed. A tall, slender man walked up the adjacent hill with the children. The figure strolled with them, an arm seemingly wrapped around each, yet such should have been impossible. Garrett blinked hard and when he looked again, he spied only the children, huddled on the hill together, on a wooden bench beneath a bent willow tree.

Amy flew up the walk and into his arms, her face as red as his cap. "Sister Constance says I have to take all the brats back with me to Sister Mary Lou."

"Wait." He took hold of her shoulders, which trembled beneath her coat. "Don't call them that."

She sniffed. "I didn't. That's what she called 'em."

He exhaled loudly. "What children?"

"Them, us, me." She gestured to the others as tears dripped down her face. "I wish my grandma Pearl would come get us."

"You have a grandmother named Pearl?" He recollected something their camp cook, Pearl, had once said—about having tended lighthouses all her life. Could it be?

"Yes, but she didn't answer Father Leo's letters. We think she's dead, like grandpa."

"Did she run a lighthouse?"

Amy wiped tears from her cheeks. "Yes, how did you know?"

A sour-faced nun, the antithesis of Sister Mary Lou, exited the building and shoved a bundle of clothes at Garrett. "The little one isn't potty trained and the eldest is fond of breaking things. The one in between doesn't speak much and won't eat our food—so don't blame us for her thin frame."

Garrett could only gape as the woman spun on her heel and returned to the building.

"I don't think God would like what she did." Amy pulled her brother's cap further down over his pink-tipped ears.

"Me neither." His heart ached that these children would be set out on the curb like refuse.

"And the man that sat out here and waited with us—he didn't like it either, but he made me promise to stay and wait for you. And he said all would be well."

"All would be well?" That was the same thing he'd heard, and felt, after he'd saved Rebecca. "I reckon it will be, then. But first, I want to go check in with your grandma, Pearl."

"You know her?"

"If she's who I think then yes, missy, I do. What was your ma's name before she got married?"

She stated Pearl's last name. "That's a ringer!"

"Yes!" Amy clapped her hands together.

"Well then, I know where your grandma is. And I'm gonna go see my Pa and share my good news about my job."

The carriage driver assisted them up.

"I reckon this is gonna cost me a might more than I paid getting here." Garrett searched his coat pocket, fingering his coins, but didn't want to count his money in front of the man.

"No, sir, in fact this entire ride is on me."

Amy gawked at the driver. "Thank you, Mr. Stan. And don't go too fast!"

The girl clung to Garrett for the rest of the ride as he bounced her brother on one knee and the other two children sat silently in the back, sucking on sugar twists that the driver had handed them.

When they got out and went to the Mackinaw City dock, Garrett handed her wriggling brother down to Amy and once again offered to pay.

"Not needed. May God bless you with what you're doing."

As the carriage departed, Amy tugged on his hand. "You should have met the man who waited with us under the tree."

So he'd not imagined the stranger. "Did you recognize him?"

"No, he must be new to the island. But he sure was nice and he smelled so good—like the incense used at mass on holy days."

A shiver worked its way under Garrett's Mackinaw jacket as he picked up the littlest child and went to purchase tickets. This was the right thing to do. He had peace about it. If these were Pearl's grandkids, she needed to make some decisions. And when she did, he wanted her to know he was making decisions of his own, too.

Chapter Ten

The bells jingled as the door opened. Rebecca jumped up from where she'd bent over a shipment of fancy buttons, dropping a card of mother-of-pearl buttons in the process. Without Garrett in the store and Amelia gone, all her fears had returned, including nightmares of Myron showing up, waiting in the shadows.

She shivered as Tom Jeffries removed his bowler hat and hung it on a peg.

"I've come to check on you and make sure all is well." If Garrett had stated those words, there'd be warmth in them—a promise of something just beneath the surface. But with Tom, she sensed the offer was one forced on him by Jo. His tone was almost as brisk as the Lake Michigan breeze that day.

She cocked her head at him, appraising the difference between the two men. Tom was handsome, but his attempts to be clever always fell short with her, whereas Garrett understated his capabilities and instead produced a level of craftsmanship she'd never seen before. "Thanks. It's been slow, other than the ladies coming to pick up their fabric and notions for new gowns for the ball."

He laughed. "That's an oxymoron. A Lumberjacks' Ball. Woodcutter's dance maybe—but a ball?"

Offense rose up in her. "You should see the fancy gowns that Sister Mary Lou is whipping up! Once you view those, you won't be looking down your nose." She was beginning to understand why Jo had thought Tom could be cocky at times.

The handsome teacher shook his head. "It just strikes me as funny. Sorry. And yes, even my own sweet fiancé will be lovely in one of Sister Mary Lou's creations."

Rebecca stretched her shoulders, hoping to ease some of the tension.

The doorbells jingled again as the door opened. The elderly dockworker limped inside. "Good day, Miss Hart." He closed the door gently behind him, scooting out of the way on his good foot.

"What is it, Charlie?"

"I was supposed to give you a message from Mr. Christy."

"Which one?"

He stroked his chin. "Only know the one fella."

Tom surprised Rebecca by pulling a chair over for the infirm man. She should have thought to do so. But Charlie shook his head. "Only here for a minute. Mr. Christy said to get word to you and his sister that he was going to see his Pa downstate."

"Is anything wrong?"

"Dunno, he just hollered that at me when he saw me at the dock on the island. I was getting my daughter settled back in at her work over there." Charlie shrugged. "Mr. Christy boarded a ship going to Mackinaw City. Looked like he was surrounded by a whole bunch of kids."

"What?" Rebecca pressed her hand to her stiff collar, which suddenly felt tight.

Tom edged toward the dockworker. "Did he say anything else? Like whether something happened to his father? I'm marrying the senior Mr. Christy's daughter, Josephine."

"Nope. And I gotta get back to work." Arching a shaggy white eyebrow, Charlie surveyed Tom. "You're marrying that pretty gal, Jo?"

"Yes." Tom stood straighter.

Shaking his head, Charlie clucked his tongue as he headed out the door, disapproval evident in the glimpse she had of his face.

Rebecca stifled the urge to chuckle out loud. She turned her face away so Tom wouldn't see her expression.

"What do you make of that?" Tom took two steps forward and looked out the window toward the docks.

"About Charlie thinking Jo might be too good for you?" He wouldn't want to hear what she had to say on that topic.

His cheeks reddened. "No, about your *sweetheart* going to see my future father-in-law?" He'd spoken the word sweetheart like an epithet, but Rebecca wasn't about to get pulled into an argument.

"I wonder if the elder Mr. Christy wanted one of his sons to take over for him because he's ill. Maybe that's why Garrett's father announced he was quitting."

"He seemed fine a month ago." Tom crossed his arms over his chest.

"Yes, well so did my locksmith!" Rebecca glared at him. "But the sheriff told me this morning that the man was found dead."

"What?" Tom drew in his chin.

"My locksmith come down with ague a few weeks back. When he didn't attend church service or open his shop, the sheriff went in there." Nausea bubbled up as she imagined what the lawman had found. "I think it's hard for the elderly to fight off sickness—especially if they don't have anyone looking after them."

"How old was he?" A crinkle formed between Tom's green eyes.

She shrugged. "He had white hair."

"Well, he sure seemed spry enough when he was traipsing up and down those stairs at the inn."

"Are we talking about the same man?" Rebecca retrieved a feather duster from beneath the counter and attacked the nearby display of tea tins with it.

"Only saw him one time, and from a distance, but he ran up to the top floor with no trouble." Tom slouched against the door and pulled his pocket watch out.

"Maybe you saw his assistant."

He eyed her. "He doesn't have one. Or didn't..."

No point in disagreeing with Tom. "Regardless, he's passed on now, which means I won't be getting that back door lock fixed unless someone comes down from Sault Ste. Marie or over from Naubinway."

"Let me take a gander at it." Tom offered what she assumed was one of his persuasive grins. "Jo says I'm handy."

Rebecca laughed. "Your good looks won't get you far with me, but Jo's recommendation will."

"Aw, come on, Rebecca, you know you're starting to warm up to me. Besides, who knows—you might end up becoming my sister-in-law."

"Don't start..." Shooting him a hard stare, she heard him snicker as he swiveled around.

"Let me double-check the back work room before I head out." As they parted the curtains, the scent of turpentine, and something else pungent, made her cough.

"Phew! What's Garrett using back here?" Tom waved a hand in front of his face and then opened the back door. "And why is this door unlocked?"

Wads of cotton lay strewn about on the floor and a box of sawdust sat propped against the wall. "This isn't like him. Garrett always keeps the room clean and neat."

With the door open, a fresh chill breeze dispersed some of the odor but Rebecca's eyes still watered. "I wish I had my workshop ready out back, but the builder said he can't complete it until the ground thaws. Which should be soon."

"Well, in the meantime, I'm taking these rags outside for you. No need for that odor in there. Not to mention, they're highly flammable." Tom made a noise of disgust.

Surely Garrett wouldn't have left them. Was he so distracted by something—or by someone—that he'd failed to clean up after himself? Jo had confided about the métis woman he'd been courting. But Jo had said she was gone. Rebecca believed, by Jo's tone, that she meant the woman had died. Had she returned to Mackinaw City? Doubt niggled at her. Was it Garrett's past or her own chasing her?

Rebecca's hands began to tremble. "Did…did Garrett tell you about what happened to me?"

"Not exactly. But he did tell me to look out for you."

☙☙☙

Mackinaw City, town

A black Labrador retriever, the size of a timber wolf, leapt from a dray and charged right at Garrett. Behind him, he heard the children's collective gasp.

"Blue Dog!" Jo's pet threw himself at Garrett's chest, and he took the dog's paws and rested them on his shoulders as the beast licked his face. Chuckling from deep in his belly, Garrett knew camp driver, Frenchie Brevort, must be in town for supplies.

"*Bonjour*!" Pearl's fiancé hotfooted it toward them. "What brings you here?"

Clapping Frenchie on the shoulder, Garrett pulled him closer and whispered in his ear, "I think these here children might be Pearl's grandchildren."

The white-haired man drew back and glanced to where Blue Dog now lay at the feet of the four children. "*Magnifique!*" He danced a little jig right there in the muddy street. "Come along, your grand-mère will be so *joyeux*."

"Sure glad you showed up, or I would have had to put this little troupe up for the night here in Mackinaw City."

"Won't your pa be surprised? Eh?" Frenchie grinned.

Amy giggled as Jo's pet rose and licked each of the children's hands.

"Kids, old Blue does that when he wants a treat, so maybe we best duck in and get him something for the drive out."

"*Oui*." Frenchie tossed Garrett a coin. "And some *bonbons* for *les enfants*. Children always like their sweets."

Garrett laughed. "I'll be right back."

He took the toddler, Jimmy, into his arms and held the other brother's hand while the two girls trailed behind them. He turned toward the dog, but Frenchie already had him jumping up into the back of the dray.

Amy's tug on his sleeve got his attention. "Mr. Christy, that man doesn't have any teeth."

"Some men ain't got any sense in their heads but possess a full set of choppers." He raised his eyebrows. "Which one do you reckon you'd prefer he has?"

She pooched out her lower lip. "I reckon you're right."

Laughing, he caught her eye. "And I reckon you don't need to be picking up my speech habits, little miss."

"Was that man French?"

"He's American, and he fought for freedom for the unfortunates who were enslaved. And that cost him a set of teeth." Children these days didn't seem to understand much. But he didn't want her or the others saying anything to the kind man who'd been like a second father to him, Moose, and Jo. How old was Frenchie anyways? Were he and Pearl going to be up to the task of child-raising?

After purchasing some chews for the dog and candy sticks for the children, he ushered them outside, again, before the busybody ladies in there could ask him any questions. "Come on now, we best be getting out to the camp before it gets dark."

A beaming Frenchie met them outside and assisted each child up into the back of the dray. "Good thing I have room. You all fit well. Just sit there and cover up." He pointed to a tall stack of wool blankets.

Ensuring that each was properly seated and bundled up, Garrett climbed up front and hopped onto the buckboard with the driver.

"Your father is doing well. Anxious to hear which *homme* will run the new camp."

"Won't be me."

The man cackled. "That's what Pearl said."

"Speaking of which, I need to ask you some things about her."

After Frenchie released the brake, he clucked his tongue and slapped the reins against the two horse's backs. "Such as?"

"Well, for one thing, where was she before she came out to the camp to cook?"

"She was at the lighthouse for a long time after her *mari*—her husband—died, until they could replace him as the keeper. She ran the place by herself for a while, but she was lonely there."

"Did she have an estranged son—one who ran off?"

"*Oui.* Odd, but she just recently had mail forwarded from the old post office near their last lighthouse. Her son had a falling out with his parents many years ago. Ran off and sailed as a *marin marchand*, how you say— merchant mariner. Never bothered visiting his *maman* again. Pearl was so heartbroken. He wrote that he owned a small store on Mackinac Island and had a wife and a *famille*. Wanted to see his parents again."

Garrett's heart sank into his stomach. He didn't want to destroy Pearl's hope. *God, what do I do? What do I say?*

The two men rode in silence, as the children chattered with one another in the back. Frenchie shook his head sadly as he directed the horses to turn onto the camp road. They had miles ahead of them, and Garrett hoped to learn more. "I sure don't want to upset your new wife. Nor you. But these here kids are her grandchildren and..."

Frenchie spit out a stream of tobacco into the muddy rutted roadway. "*Orphelins?*"

"Yes, orphans."

"*C'est dommage.* What a shame. Pearl and her son could have reconciled before he died."

They traveled on into the woods. Here and there fresh green grass and buds strained to start a new spring. By the time they arrived at the logging camp, Garrett knew what he had to do. He explained to Frenchie, who took the children to his cabin, and then sought out Pearl at the cook house.

The familiar scent of pine, woodsmoke, biscuits, ham, and baked apples brought on a powerful hunger not only for the food but for the fellowship of the other lumberjacks and their families, as well as his own. But Moose wasn't there, and Jo and Tom were gone, too. Moisture blurred his vision and he blinked. Must have been misting rain outside and he'd not noticed. He strode up the narrow aisle between the long tables set with red and white checked oilcloth, just as they'd been several months earlier.

Nothing had changed, except him. In two weeks, he'd be at the Grand Hotel constructing cabinets, armoires, and bed frames. He'd be residing in nearby in a small house with enough room for a wife and even visitors, or children should he be so blessed. The woman who immediately came to mind—would she entertain the notion of marrying a former lumberjack?

Lord, watch over Rebecca while I'm gone. And over Moose and Jo and Tom, too.

⌘

Rebecca sucked in a deep breath and then exhaled slowly as Tom constructed a wooden make-shift bar to secure the back door. "Are you sure this is a good idea?"

"If you mean this extra latch, then yes." He slid the rectangular piece of oak down and into place, which would safeguard the door from entry. "If you mean about going to Mackinaw City, yes, again—but that's Jo's good idea, and this is mine."

Again he offered her his half-grin, which always seemed to make Jo acquire a silly grin, but just made Rebecca shake her head at the man's attempt to charm. That was something she loved about Garrett—he never tried that stuff on her. Honest, direct, and simple about what he did, Garrett made no attempts to manipulate people or influence them unless he felt it was for their own good. She loved his quiet manner when he worked on wood so intently, sanding down and finishing off until the object shone its most perfect patina. And he'd impressed her with his emotional constraint and because he didn't flirt with the women in the shop. Even when those examining his armoires, for purchase, would bat their eyes and giggle, he ignored their behavior. She loved how he… She loved *him*.

But something in her gut seemed to shatter into a million pieces that cut into her. She bent over, feeling the sensation that she knew wasn't from a true physical ailment.

"You all right, Rebecca?"

Go.

She looked up at Tom but knew he hadn't urged her. And her body screamed that she should stay here—let Jo and Tom find Garrett and Amelia. She'd stay and prove that she could manage this store and look after herself without anyone else's help.

Trust.

Look what trust had gotten her with Myron, who at this very moment may be trying to kill her. She was being silly. Just because Garrett had failed to clean up his work space one time. And hadn't locked the door, she was overreacting.

Obey.

Shivers coursed down her body to her boots. *God, show me that is You. Please help me trust and obey.*

"You're shaking." Tom took hold of her shoulders. "You're going to just need to trust God and go with us."

She stared at him. Yes. She would trust and obey.

And Lord, may my actions be blessed by You.

Chapter Eleven

Christy Lumber Camp, outside Mackinaw City

Pearl and Frenchie gathered the children around the potbelly stove in their shack as Garrett retrieved extra wood to feed the fire. The night had turned cool. He hoped Rebecca had gotten his message in St. Ignace and hadn't worried.

"Is that really you, Ox?" Ruth's sweet voice carried across the clearing.

Sven trailed after her, toward Garrett, both of their boots kicking up the piney muck that covered the central camp area. He'd forgotten how dirty his boots got and how long it took to clean them off at night. But he had recalled that shanty boys didn't bathe as often as he now did, which was another reason he'd chosen to stay in Pa's cabin.

"*Ja,* it truly is you." Sven threw out a wide hand and grasped Garrett's with such force that his knees almost buckled. "You getting soft on us, Ox?"

Sven laughed and Garrett did, too. His old friend could say such "fighting words" to his face, but he'd never spread rumors nor would he make nasty remarks behind his back.

"How are your wedding plans coming, you two lovebirds?"

Ruth shrugged. "Soon as we get settled in the new camp, if..."

"Your Pa says he's for quitting this kind of work." Sven's light eyebrows joined together.

The pretty blond leaned toward Garrett. "Honestly, your Pa's notion started when Tom's aunt showed up."

"His aunt?" Cordelia's sister must have arrived and like her had shown up out of the blue, too.

"Yes. And she's just as pretty as Mrs. Jeffries."

Garrett frowned. "What is she doing here, and what has this got to do with my Pa?"

Sven patted his stomach. "Been cooking for us."

Rolling her eyes, Ruth elbowed Sven. "Mrs. St. Clair came to see if her sister needed help at the inn, but your Pa convinced her that he was desperate for help here, with Jo gone."

"How long has she been here? Cordelia acted as though she'd just heard from her."

After playfully punching at Garrett's shoulder, Sven laughed. "She's been here long enough, my friend, ja?"

"Irene is a sweetheart—we just love her in the kitchen."

Still chuckling, Sven mumbled, "More than just the cooks feel that way."

Ruth brought a booted heel down on Sven's instep and he howled. She shook her head. "Forgive my fiancé, he seems to be feeling his oats today. But as I was going to say, who can understand sisters and why they do what they do?"

"Not me, that's for sure." Garrett eyed his father's cabin, which loomed so empty without Jo's presence.

Ruth sighed. "I think Irene is embarrassed at all the attention your Pa is paying to her."

"Ja, you should see them." Sven squeezed Ruth's hand. "I think they might have their own plans."

"So Pa may marry this woman?" Garrett shook his head as though he could dispel cobwebs from between his ears. "Is that what you've been beatin' all around the bush about?"

"Ja, but we hear you have your own news." Sven waggled his eyebrows.

Had he heard about Rebecca? "Oh?" He hadn't even begun courting her much less asked her to marry him.

"You won't be with us up North—Moose may be boss."

"I don't think Moose is mature enough to manage the camp." Garrett allowed his opinion to sit there between him and Sven, like an unclaimed biscuit on the counter.

Both Sven and Ruth remained silent, the sound of squealing children, in the distance, carrying through the pine trees.

Sven cleared his throat, then glanced to Ruth and then to Garrett. "But I can help Moose manage, ja?"

Garrett pulled his friend into a brief bear hug and then released him. "You betcha."

"Ox, I don't want to cook up there, though. I thought you should know." Ruth's gaze moved to the tree line, from where her siblings emerged. "I'll be staying at home."

How would Rebecca manage if he were to marry her and if they took in the orphans? That was, if Pearl and Frenchie couldn't manage them. He'd have to chew on that notion for a while. Of course, it would help if Rebecca Jane actually developed any interest in marrying him…

"Good news for me—I've got a job doing cabinetry on Mackinac Island."

Ruth squealed. "That's so exciting. Congratulations!" She kissed his cheek.

Sven pulled her back to his side. "Ja, we know you want this new work a long time. Best wishes." He extended his hand.

"Thanks." Garrett accepted Sven's handshake.

This entire exchange with his friend reminded Garrett of one of the last serious conversations they'd had about life and where it was taking them. Misty Fawn had accepted his offer of marriage and Sven expressed his concerns. They were valid, for many of the lumberjacks held strong prejudices against the Chippewa and Odawa who populated the area. But within the month, the beautiful métis widow and her children had died from an illness so virulent it struck down a quarter of the small village where she lived outside the lumber camp. Too numb with shock to properly grieve, it had taken his mother's death, after Misty Fawn's and the children's, to finally open that wound and let it heal. He and Pa mourned in private, together, far more than Jo or Moose had ever known.

Pa strolled toward them, a tall brunette, bearing a strong resemblance to the striking Cordelia Jeffries, on his arm. This must be Irene. Pa patted the woman's hand before releasing her arm from his. He then closed the distance between himself and Garrett. Grinning broadly, he opened his arms, and with a bear hug lifted him briefly off his feet. "Don't say yer old man can't still do that, son. And what are they feedin' you over there? Ya feel like ya lost some weight."

After Pa set him down on solid ground, Garrett playfully punched him in the arm. "Ain't lumberjacking no more. Don't need all those vittles that Jo and the ladies served up." *And Ma, too had done, God rest her soul.*

The pretty stranger flushed beneath Garrett's appraisal. She indeed was a handsome woman, but what was Pa doing already seeking out another wife? Maybe with him knocking on fifty years' door soon, he didn't want to be alone. Still, it grated a bit.

With a flip of his wrist, Pa gestured the woman toward him. "I want you to meet Cordelia's sister, Mrs. Irene St. Clair."

Cordelia had mentioned the widow recently. "Happy to know you, ma'am. Your sister sure is lookin' forward to seeing you soon." But with the way Pa and her seemed so cozy, was Cordelia's hope misplaced that her sister would soon join her in the Upper Peninsula?

"Good to see you, Garrett." Mrs. St. Clair smiled up at him. "I can't wait to catch up with Cordelia when we make the move."

She and Pa exchanged a long glance. Garrett squelched the urge to question them.

"Looks like my boy got himself shaved." Pa laughed. "Makes him look younger, which goes along with that leaner look he's sportin' now."

Garrett ran his hand along his now-stubbled jawline. At the end of most days, he needed to shave before dinner, but such wouldn't be needed here. He shot his father a look but ignored his comment as he addressed Irene. "Nice meeting you, too, ma'am." His face itched, but he resisted the urge to scratch his chin.

Pa scrunched up his face like one of Ma's cornhusk dolls. "You gonna keep clean shaven, son? Or are you gonna let your beard grow back in?"

"Pa, this is one day's growth." Garrett sighed and then hated himself for doing so. He was a grown man, not a kid anymore. "Gonna keep myself shaved, but I ain't got a razor here. So, yes sir, I suspect by tomorrow I could have the beginnings of a new beard."

The lady blushed, as though this topic was too intimate for her to overhear. "Come, come, Mr. Christy, let's not embarrass him."

Pa laughed. "Let the barber get you in town before you cross back over, son."

"We'll see." Garrett felt all of twelve years old again.

"I'm assuming you got yourself some good work lined up, then." Pa winked at him. "Given this new hankerin' for a smooth face."

"Yessir."

"Don't you worry none about your brother—he'll do just fine." Pa clapped him on the shoulder then grinned at Sven. "You boys got a good friend in Sven. And I've got me a new camp assistant for your brother. So yer off the hook, Ox."

Garrett smiled and cringed at the same time. "About that nickname, sir…"

Chapter Twelve

As Rebecca, Tom, and Jo entered the queue for the ferry, Charlie hobbled out from one of the buildings that held shipments and baggage bordering the docks. His features tugged in several directions. "Miss Hart, I need to tell ya something."

Tom cocked an eyebrow at her.

"What is it, Charlie?" She offered him a smile.

"I, uh, I got your message about keeping your shipments."

"Good."

Jo tapped her toe as the infirm man removed his cap and twisted it in his gnarled hands.

"And Miss Christy, I'm supposed to tell you that your brother acquired a good-payin' job at the Grand Hotel."

Her friend beamed. "Good news."

The porter slapped his cap back on. "Miss Hart, I fear that means you'll lose your fine carpenter."

"Yes." *Much more than a carpenter.* Rebecca's spirits plummeted.

Charlie departed and Jo took her hand. "Don't look so down. I know you care for Garrett and I believe he does for you, too."

Tom moved ahead, allowing them privacy, as he toted their bags to the ferry attendants.

Rebecca ran her tongue over her dry lips. "Does…is…the woman Garrett was to wed…"

Jo stopped walking and pulled Rebecca from the line of those departing. "Didn't I tell you that the poor dear and her children died?

"No."

"It was years ago, but Little Fawn and all her children died when illness struck her tribe."

How tragic. Rebecca's heart clenched. Here she was begrudging that Garrett may return to his lost love and the poor woman was departed to her heavenly home. A passenger's cane grazed her leg, and Rebecca jumped back. Jo held Rebecca's hand, preventing her from falling over a trunk, behind her, and pulled her upright.

"Oh, my, Rebecca, you best settle down before you end up overboard." Jo released her hands but then linked her arm with hers. "It has been almost two years since Misty Fawn died. And she was a believer, as were her children. That gives me consolation as I hope it did Garrett."

"You're not sure that faith helps Garrett?"

Jo ducked her chin to her chest but then met Rebecca's eyes. "Something happened that got between him and God. About ten years ago something really bad happened. And he's not been the same faithful boy he was."

"He's a man now." Had her plight caused Garrett's beliefs to falter? That had been a decade earlier.

Jo laughed. "Yes, he seemed to become a man overnight. And it's only recently that he says he relishes time spent in the Word and listens to the sermons—asks questions afterwards."

"So he's coming back to the Lord." Relief coursed through Rebecca.

"I believe so." Jo released her arm so the two could board the boat.

Soon they were underway, and Tom obtained hot tea and sweet rolls for them. "Not as good as my fiancé's, but close."

Jo gazed up at Tom with a look that Rebecca hoped would one day pass between Garrett and herself. Hadn't she already glimpsed him making eyes like that at her when she'd entered the back room of the mercantile? Her cheeks heated at the memory. But if he'd already procured employment on the island, what could that mean? Still, she felt a blessed peace such as she'd not experienced in a long while.

She sat back in her seat, listening to Tom and Jo's comments and bits of conversation from the other passengers. One lady sought out her daughter to bring garments she'd knit for a grandchild. An older gentleman planned to visit the tavern to hear the latest songstress brought in for the summer season. All around her, people were making plans and connecting with their loved ones and engaging in activities they enjoyed. Why shouldn't she as well? The burden of running the shop lifted, freedom beckoned.

Soon coming to an end, the trip across the straits exhilarated Rebecca in a way she'd forgotten, so long had it been since she'd loosened the stiff bindings she kept on her emotions. The deep blue and then aquamarine tones of water gave way to a misty gray-green as they reached the docks in Mackinaw City. Seagulls swooped down to gobble up crumbs that the very earliest tourists and returning summer folk had scattered on the park banks.

After they'd disembarked and taken sustenance at a small café, Tom sought transportation for them. When he returned, an older man, whose head reached Tom's shoulder, accompanied him.

As Jo introduced Rebecca, her eyes twinkled. "Frenchie, this is Rebecca Hart."

"Enchanté." Old world charm emanated from the elderly lumberjack despite his rustic appearance. He swept off his slouch hat and bowed as though they were at court in France.

"Frenchie is my Pa's camp driver."

"Oui, I am glad I made this second trip this week to town."

"Thank you for driving us."

"I brought Garrett, as he now wishes to be called, out to camp last night, with the children."

Tom made a shooing motion toward the ancient dray, parked on the street. "Time to move along, ladies."

Frenchie took Jo's arm and escorted her out to the street, Tom's scowling face making Rebecca stifle a giggle. The Frenchman pointed to the back of the most dilapidated wagon Rebecca had seen in some time, its wood sides grayed to almost silver. "Was in town for more supplies for Pearl's grandchildren and the celebration tonight."

Jo tapped his arm. "What grandchildren?"

"I'll tell you on the way, but we must get going." He held out his hand.

Light rain seeped through Rebecca's new red-and-black jacket, a close-fitting garment that would easily become soaked through if true rain commenced.

"All right." Jo handed Tom her bag.

"Hop on up, *Mademoiselle* Josephine." The driver assisted Jo into the front seat. "We will head to the Christy camp, as quickly as we can, ahead of this rain."

Rebecca vowed she wouldn't complain as the raindrops thickened and blotted into her pretty jacket that would surely cling to her before long.

"Frenchie, where are the lap robes?" Jo stood up front, arms akimbo.

Rebecca nibbled her lip and kept her head down as townspeople gawked at them loading onto the dray. What would her mother say if she could see her now? She'd die of embarrassment.

The elderly driver moved to the back and retrieved two dusty Hudson Bay woolen blankets and handed them up. Rebecca sneezed.

"God bless you. I'll sit in the back, but let me help you up, first." Tom grabbed her around her waist and hoisted her up before she could stop him.

Jo rolled her eyes. "He's just showing off his muscles."

Leaning in, Rebecca whispered, "Which will rapidly disappear if he remains teaching."

They giggled and, after Rebecca settled on the buckboard, Jo spread a lap robe over the two of them. Sun peeked through the clouds and the rain altered to a gentle mist.

When the driver mounted, Jo passed him a blanket but he shook his head. "You're looking *belle*, Josephine."

Jo patted her auburn curls, made bouncier by the rain. "I have a maid, a butler, my own chef, and a wardrobe of beautiful gowns now."

"At the inn?" The man's mouth gaped open, revealing no teeth. *Poor thing.*

With a laugh, Jo tapped him on his arm. "No, but Tom says I have the handsomest fiancé in all of Michigan."

This drew a snort from the elderly man. Obviously he knew Tom well. He released the brake and directed the horses to move out into the thoroughfare. Few carriages populated the roadway, but soon the trains would be loaded with tourists and summer residents of Mackinac Island. Those wealthy people would be dressed in finery shipped from Paris or London, not from small shops such as hers or her parents. No matter how hard her parents had tried to climb the social ladder in their small city, they'd never attracted this type of clientele. Now, here was their daughter riding out in an ancient dray to a lumber camp. But, indeed, she did wear a lovely new jacket, one that would match the red-and-black checks of the lumberjacks' flannel shirts.

In all her years of waiting on lumberjacks, Rebecca Jane had never actually gone to visit any of the camps. They'd set up two different stores, moving northward as the camps did, a little over a decade each time. But in neither case had she ventured to see what life was really like, although she'd heard many tales. More horrible stories when they were further south.

Jo squeezed her hand. "Won't Garrett be surprised?"

Surprised wasn't the emotion she'd hope for. *Pleased. Delighted. Enthused.*

Maybe it wasn't God nudging her on this trip. Surely, this had to be a mistake. She'd abandoned her new mercantile and traipsed across the straits of Mackinac with Jo and Tom and for what reason? Garrett had made no promises to her. He'd not even indicated that he cared for her, even though she'd seen it in his eyes. She'd cut him off whenever he steered their conversation in that direction and maybe she'd been wrong. Maybe all those times he wanted to talk about them, he'd just wanted to tell her he was moving and intended to live elsewhere.

Trust. Obey. Release.

That had to be God speaking to her heart, because this folly wasn't compatible with her intellect. She sighed as the driver urged the horses to merge behind a sporting light carriage.

"I think that must belong to one of the summer folk." Jo cocked her head, gazing at the jaunty carriage with fringe dangling from its cover.

Rebecca shivered. "I wish summer would arrive soon." She needed those tourists to keep coming across the straits to make purchases at her store and to bring her accounts out of the red.

As Frenchie and Jo chatted in low tones, Rebecca found herself lulled by the gentle breeze, the creaking of the wagon wheels, and the clip-clopping of the horses' hooves. Before she knew it, they were deep in the fragrant piney woods, so heavily canopied that it almost seemed like dusk. Along they jostled, wildlife periodically crossing their path. The driver kept a gun nearby. "For bears and all," he'd said. But Rebecca's stomach sickened to think that a worse and more dangerous creature was Myron Peevey.

"I'm sure glad my Pa is okay." Jo shivered under the blanket, and Rebecca covered her gloved hand with her own. "I was trying to keep up a cheerful front but I'm not a very good actress."

She smiled at Jo, whose red-rimmed eyes announced that she'd been crying before their journey that day. "What did we tell you? All will be well." As she hoped it would be, with Garrett.

"I'm so glad you decided to come with us. I can't even explain why I was so insistent you had to come." Jo rubbed her head. "I'm not normally such a pesterer, and Tom was coming with me, too."

"Tom urged me to come, too." As well as the Holy Spirit.

Jo exhaled loudly. "I am so grateful Frenchie could give us a ride."

The older man grinned. "Wait till you see Pearl's grandchildren. She's so caught up with them that she can't think straight, and she's so grateful to your brother, Jo. Garrett brought them straight away."

Rebecca leaned forward. "Mr. Brevort, who are these grandchildren?"

A smile lit Jo's pretty face. "Frenchie says that Amy and her brothers and sister are Pearl's grandchildren—but she'd never seen them before."

"Never? That's so sad."

"I know."

"But my little shop helper has a grandmother?"

"Oui. And a *grand-père*, Miss Hart. *Moi.*" He gave the reins a little flick and the horses pulled swiftly down the rutted bone-jarring road. "And I'm guessin' now that you must be Ox's wife-to-be. Amy told us about you and your shop."

Rebecca's breath stuck in her chest until the next hard bump got her lungs working again. Wife to be? As far as she knew, he planned to go on to the island without her. And she couldn't bear that.

But she would face this challenge head on and not run.

Chapter Thirteen

W e need to talk, Pa." Garrett wrung his cap in his hands, feeling like it, and he, would fall apart if he didn't get this off his chest. "You know I didn't want to disappoint you. And I'm grateful you've brought Sven in to help run the new camp."

"Have a seat." Pa snaked his foot around the nearby chair and, hooking it, pulled it closer to where he sat. "Is this about Misty Fawn? You can't blame yourself. And you shouldn't blame God."

Garrett's mouth went dry. "My beef with God started well before Misty Fawn and her children died. Before Ma's passing."

Pa snapped open his tobacco box and filled his pipe. "About the time you saved Miss Daggenhart, I reckon."

"Yes, sir."

His father cocked his head at him. "Not wondering about your beliefs, are you? I can bear up under you leaving the lumber camps, but please don't tell me you're abandoning your faith. Just lost one of our new men to pneumonia, and I fear he'd abandoned his faith. Weighs on me heavy that he may not have gone to heaven."

"No, sir."

"Good. That's somethin' a parent always worries about with their children." Pa tamped some tobacco down in his corncob pipe. "And I've continued to pray for you even in my own dark times after your mother died."

Garrett nodded and leaned forward. "I started praying for all of us again about that time, too."

His father arched his dark eyebrows at him. "Just because that boy almost killed the girl you had sights on—that doesn't mean God had it in for you or your loved ones."

"I know..." Garrett rocked onto the chair's back legs. "And I need to talk with you about that." He had to tell him about Rebecca and his intentions toward her and about his new job.

"About how you finally could give up that job of thinking you could keep everyone safe? The job I never assigned to you and Moose, of watching all the time over Jo?"

This wasn't the job he planned on discussing. "Maybe I've finally given up that task. I know that God can conquer any enemy." Even now, though, he worried that by being away from Rebecca he endangered her safety from Peevey, if the wretch was out there looking for her.

"God can do that, son, not you—you don't have to think your fists will find a solution to every giant stumbling through the land."

"Or every crazy murderous lumberjack out there—you're right." Thank God he and Richard had been in the right place at the right time.

Where I wanted you.

"Huh?" Pa looked around almost as though he'd heard the words, too. He frowned as he lit his pipe. "You think you're the new sheriff up there or something? Can't you just let others and God do their job?"

Garrett had to grin at the rebuke—it was so true. "I guess I could trust God. He saved Daniel in the lion's den."

"God did."

"Daniel trusted."

"Exactly."

The scent of tobacco smoke filled the tiny room and brought a memory. The merchants adjacent to Rebecca's shop came out back, but there had *never* been any pipe smoke. Yet twice Garrett had found what looked like tobacco leaves at the mercantile and what Amy and Rebecca suggested was only tealeaves. What if they weren't? He struggled to hold onto his peace. *Dear God, if Rebecca is in danger, keep her safe.*

"God can seal the lions' mouths and He can free those in chains."

God wouldn't free someone like Peevey, but the prison system in Michigan had. Garrett had struggled with releasing his own shame over failing to help Misty Fawn and the children when they were so ill. He could rationalize that he and the crew were too busy with a big job bringing down trees. And the messenger had downplayed the severity of their illness. It wasn't until later that Garrett realized the man held fast to prejudice against the Indians and couldn't care less if another family of them died. If only Garrett had known. But by the time he did, Pa had warned the man to hightail it out of town lest Garrett get his hands on him. He should forgive that misbegotten, hard-hearted soul. And forgive himself and let God back into his life. It hadn't been that God couldn't reach him; it was that Garrett hadn't invited God back into his heart—really into his life and not just via a preacher on Sundays. To her last breath, Ma had believed God's will was best if they could only trust.

"Gotta tell you, boy, I was right surprised to see you walk into camp holding hands with those children. I steeled myself for a confession from you even though I believed your Ma and I had done our best to bring you up right. I had to trust."

Garrett laughed. "Pa, now you can't seriously think I'd hidden four kids off somewhere—especially with Misty Dawn having the two, that were to be mine." Who had never had a chance to be his to raise.

Inhaling the tobacco, Pa closed his eyes for a moment then fixed his dark gaze on Garrett. "Boy, I've seen more surprising things in my day. But that isn't what we were talking about. I've seen God do some flat-out miracles, too. I thought for sure you children would be convicted in your faith by some of what has happened in this here camp."

"Like when we thought old Jacob was dead?"

Pa's eyes widened. "Doc said he was. Covered him up with a sheet."

"Then the next morning Jake showed up in the breakfast line and Ma fell out."

"Eight stitches on the back of her head."

They both grew silent for a moment. If God could restore a dead man— and He'd done so with Lazarus, too—then what couldn't he do?

A chill shot straight down his backbone. "Pa, I've been offered a wonderful chance on Mackinac Island."

Chuckling, Pa cupped his pipe in his hand. "Don't reckon they have much lumber coming off that island. Especially since we hauled a bunch over for that fancy hotel a few years back—remember that?"

"Yes, sir, and that hotel is where I'll be employed."

"Tell me about it." Grinning, Pa patted Garrett's shoulder, much like his Irish grandfather always had. "Your ma would be so proud of you. And I am, too."

"And Pa—that girl I saved." His mouth suddenly became dry.

"Pretty little thing—so sad…"

"I'm gonna marry her." *If she accepts.*

"Do *what*?"

"She lives in St. Ignace—has her own little shop that her pa set her up in."

"That ornery so-and-so—I don't believe it. A stingier man I've never seen than old Daggenhart."

Was Rebecca lying? "She's been running it nigh on two months—since I've been up there. I made her cabinets."

"Thought you were helping Cordelia."

"I did. I have." This was going a little harder than he thought.

"Speaking of which, I need to share something with you, too, son."

Garrett nodded, but he already knew what was coming. His father was clearly smitten with Cordelia's sister. "Yes, sir, but I need you to know I plan to marry her as soon as possible."

Someone rapped on the door. Sven ducked his head inside. "More company, ja? Come see."

Outside, their wretched old dray pulled alongside the cook shack. Frenchie was back with Jo, Tom, and a lady whose fancy red jacket stood out like a drowning squirrel in an apple barrel, her golden brown hair trailing curls over one shoulder and swept up under a fancy little cap that dipped over her eyes. *Rebecca Jane Daggenhart.* And although that little coat revealed her womanly figure in ways that a man should find pleasing, an ugly beast of jealousy attacked Garrett right there in the center of the yard.

This was *his* woman.

ೞ

How amazing that after years of being stuck in a back room by herself, God had called Rebecca out into this group of friends. Tom offered his arms after he'd assisted Jo down from the dray. As her feet met the ground, a tall blond man gaped at them and ran to a cabin next to the cookhouse, where they'd stopped. The scents of roast pork, biscuits, and apple and cinnamon wafted toward them, making her mouth water.

A door opened at a hut across the clearing and Amelia emerged, her arms wrapped around a white-haired woman.

"That's Pearl." Jo pointed at the elderly lady.

Pearl clutched a toddler and the hand of a little girl. Another boy trailed after them as they headed toward the cookhouse.

"Rebecca!" In the other direction, Garrett ran toward them, shaking out a large Mackinaw coat as he did so.

Reaching her, Garrett hoisted her up under her arms and spun her around and around, like a small child, the Mackinaw whirling over her shoulder. When he set her down, she was dizzy and leaned into him, pressing her face against his broad chest.

He wrapped the heavy wool coat around her.

"What are you doing?"

"I love you, Rebecca Jane." He pulled the jacket up around her shoulders.

The chocolate brown of his eyes disappeared into the broad band of black as his pupils widened. Right there, in front of everyone, he kissed her, his lips warm and firm over hers. Another presence joined them, warming them. Two shall become one. Rebecca found herself lost in the intensity of emotion that flowed through her. Garrett gently broke the kiss and leaned his forehead against hers.

He pressed his bristled cheek against hers but then stepped away, leaving cool air between them and a promise in his eyes of more kisses to come. He lifted a curl that trailed down her bodice. "I like your hair like this."

She shivered at his touch. "I thought it was time I stopped hiding."

"I'm glad. You're far too lovely a lady to keep in those drab colors."

Frowning, she made to shrug off the wool coat.

"Oh no, for now, though, I want you hiding those curves of yours beneath a looser jacket." He leaned in and whispered into her ear. "We may be in a family lumber camp, but we've got plenty of single men whose eyes are perfectly fine."

Heat rushed to her cheeks. But she'd not blame herself for any attention she received. Her days of allowing Myron to destroy her confidence were over. She removed the jacket and passed it back to Garrett. "I'm responsible for my behavior as they are for their own. Just because they are lumberjacks gives them no cause to believe they can ogle me." Or harm her.

His lower lip puckered. "You're right." He drew in a deep breath but didn't exhale the sigh he sometimes did when she frustrated him. Movement behind him caught her attention. He swiveled around, and then wrapped an arm around her.

"I want you to meet…"

She'd recognize Mr. Christy anywhere. Striding toward them, sunlight glistened on silver strands that now streaked his dark hair, but he was the same broad-shouldered, square-jawed lumber camp boss who had frequented the mercantile all those years ago.

"Why, this must be Janie Daggenhart all grown up." He grinned at her, his eyes almost identical to Garrett's.

"Good to see you, sir." And it was. This man had raised the two boys who had saved her life.

Mr. Christy directed his attention to Garrett. "You couldn't have picked a prettier girl to marry."

Marry? All Garrett had said was that he loved her. Her cheeks heated as Garrett winked at her and nodded. That was his idea of a marriage proposal? She widened her eyes and gave him a tight smile she hoped conveyed her meaning—*they'd speak later*.

Jo cleared her throat and her father winked before he hugged her. "And Tom here has my beautiful daughter."

"I'm Sven. You might remember me from town." The blond man pointed to the cookhouse. "Ja, and I've got a lovely girl, too, and she's in there cooking for all of us."

Her sweetheart laughed. "We're all blessed with beauties." Garrett pulled Rebecca closer. "I've got a wonderful job on the island and even a little place with room enough for a small family."

She wanted to spend the rest of her life with him, but having him simply state what he had set up and then dictating to her would never work. Rebecca tapped him on his flannel-covered chest. "What about my store?"

He puffed out his cheeks as he exhaled. "Why don't we let God figure that out for us?"

Mr. Christy cocked his head at them. "Those are some pretty wise words, son."

"Thanks, Pa."

A stream of bearded lumberjacks began to flow from a large rectangular building, across the yard, toward them. Cat calls and whistles ensued.

"Ox!" "Jo!" "Tom!"

In minutes, they were surrounded by a huge group of men and Rebecca's breath caught in her chest. She wasn't afraid. Not anymore. Thank God. *Thank you, Jesus.* Surely it couldn't be true. Going into a lumber camp hadn't made Myron the evil man he'd become.

That was his own doing.

Chapter Fourteen

Whoops of laughter accompanied the wild dancing in the lumber camp as Tom Jeffries played his fiddle. This was no full-blown Lumberjacks' Ball, but the spontaneous dance was the most fun Rebecca could remember having. Garrett swung her round and round until she was so dizzy she tugged at his hands and pulled him to the side near one of the small campfires that surrounded the circle.

"I have to rest."

"I'm winded, too," he confessed as he plunked down on a large chunk of log, fashioned into a stool. He patted the one beside him and she sat.

Amelia ran over and tried to drag Sven up and away from Ruth because he'd sat out the last two dances. As the big Swedish man and her little blonde helper hurried out into the clearing, Rebecca exhaled in contentment. This seemed so right. Amelia's grandmother and her husband joined them, amidst another round of hooting and hollering. Frenchie Brevort gave a toothless grin as Pearl lifted her skirts and performed a jig around him. Amelia imitated as Sven clapped in time to the music.

Garrett took her hand in his, the warmth a comfort to her. "Are you enjoying yourself, sweetheart?"

She cocked her head at him. "If I truly am your sweetheart, then yes, I am."

Laughing, he bent and kissed her cheek. "You've always been the one for me, Rebecca Jane Daggenhart."

She met his direct gaze, so full of promise, firelight flickering in his chocolate eyes.

He squeezed her hand. "If I have my way, you'll be Rebecca Jane Christy or just Mrs. Garrett Christy soon enough."

Slowly, she drew in a breath filled with the scent of woodsmoke, Garrett's hair tonic, her own perfume, and hot apple cider, which heated over a nearby fire. "Maybe it's okay to put Jane back in my name. It took a long time to get everyone calling me by my first name."

"Janie was a right special girl—part of who you are and nothing at all to be ashamed of." He placed two calloused fingers beneath her chin. "Look at me and tell me you can leave that behind you and let us have a new life— the one I believe God planned from the beginning—until satan got in our way."

"In our way?" She wasn't sure what he meant.

"I had a hankering to court you for a long time before I asked your pa. And then you sent me right out your mercantile door when I asked you out." He laughed now, but she knew he'd been hurt by what he'd erroneously believed to be true—that she'd rejected him.

"Trust me, if I misunderstand you again, I'm going to get one of Jo's wooden spoons and I'll chase you down and threaten you with it if you don't clarify what you mean."

Suddenly, he drew her into his strong arms, and planted a lingering hot kiss on her mouth. Everything seemed to disappear except for him, and her, and this embrace and kiss. He tasted of the cider they'd enjoyed earlier and of the sweet promise of love fulfilled.

∞

Sweet Punkin'! He could kiss this girl every night until the day he died. Overhead, the same constellation shone as it had that night a decade earlier when he and Moose had rescued her—the night he and his brother had gone fishing in the AuSable River. He'd missed the Lumberjacks' Ball, too upset by Janie's apparent dismissal of him to attend. Ten long years had passed. He wouldn't let the next ten be without her. If she couldn't or wouldn't move to the island, then he'd have to make something work in St. Ignace. Either he'd find work in town or continue to serve as a lumberjack in his pa's camp.

He pulled back, reluctantly releasing her.

"Oh my." Rebecca's flushed face and sparkling eyes told him what he wanted to know—she felt the same way about him as he did toward her. If he had his way, they'd be married soon and there would be a family started within the year. But that was God's providence, not his—something he was only now really beginning to understand.

"I don't want to press you, Rebecca, but please pray about Pearl's suggestion. If she and Frenchie moved to the island with the girls and if you joined me there, as my wife, we could help each other."

She shrugged and pulled her shawl up around her shoulders. "If they came to St. Ignace and we were all there together, that could work, too. Right?"

He blew out a puff of air. "Yes, but I ask you to pray about it." In his heart, he already saw them living in that cozy island cottage, with Pearl and Frenchie and the children living down the street from them.

"I'd have to talk with my father about it, too, Garrett. He's expecting me to make a strong start with the store."

He didn't have a peaceful feeling in his spirit about what exactly Mr. Daggenhart's motives were. "Does he intend to have you manage it on your own?"

Another dance ended, and Tom switched to a mournful rendition of Kentucky Winder, one of Ma's favorite songs. Garrett's mother had loved him so much. What would it have been like to have a ma and pa like Rebecca's—so cold, so businesslike?

"Not exactly." Her top two pearly teeth nibbled on her lower lip. "My father said that I should find a manager or a…" She looked up with wide eyes.

"Or what?"

"A husband. But I'm sure he was joking." She stared down at her hands, now clasped so tightly in her lap that the knuckles were turning white.

"So he had no intention of moving him and your mother up North?"

"That's what I don't know, because I thought this was supposed to be *my* store and my new start. But…"

"But what?" He covered her hands with his.

"Well, he kept talking about how he felt the lumber trade was moving north."

"True enough."

"And that moving to the Upper Peninsula might be the wisest thing to do if income continued to fall at the mercantile in the Lower Peninsula."

"And had it?"

"I think so. But it doesn't make sense that he'd tell me one thing and then plan on doing another."

"Rebecca, your pa has never made sense to me. Him and your ma dressing you up like a doll but then paying you no never mind when you needed some real attention. Then what you're telling me about them shoving you off to the back rooms after the attack. What kind of parent does that?"

"Not a good one." Pain reflected on her beautiful face. "And I don't want to be like them."

A flash of red blazed across the dance area as Amy chased Ruth's little sister. Frenchie helped Pearl up from a nearby log. They might be spry for their ages, but how would they keep up with all those kids?

They sat silently as the dancers swirled around in the clearing. Tom fiddled with gusto, breaking to loud applause. Then he began to play a mournful tune Garrett didn't recognize. The sadness contained in the music caused moisture to build in Garrett's eyes and beside him Rebecca openly cried. He wrapped an arm around her and pulled her to his side then kissed the top of her head. Despite the absence of fripperies in the camp, somehow she'd manage to have her hair curled and arranged into an elaborate mass of ringlets. Jo had kept her by the kitchen house fire for an hour, using hot tongs. Rebecca did look beautiful. But he'd have thought her just fine even if she wore her hair up in the severe bun she'd preferred.

"If my mother and father do come up to take over the store, I won't abide it." Her tone was determined, her features set. "I'd have to leave."

"Do you enjoy the work?" She rarely smiled when she was at the shop— not unless Amy had come to help. "You don't seem real happy there."

Slowly, ever so slowly, like the slow falling of a gigantic tree freshly cut, Rebecca turned to look up at him. She laughed and the chuckles built until she was crying.

"What is so dadburned funny?"

"No, Garrett." She wrapped her arms across her torso as she continued to laugh. "I do not enjoy the work, but I'm persistent if I'm anything."

"Now that's a true statement if ever there was one. You were always steadfast in anything you undertook."

She shook her head. "And that's a bad characteristic if it's just me being obstinate in pursuing something that wasn't mine to begin with."

"Well then, Miss Rebecca Jane, I believe we're getting closer to our answer."

Chapter Fifteen

After Garrett awoke in the morning, he washed, dressed in his town clothes, and enjoyed the hearty breakfast of biscuits, gravy, eggs, potatoes, and bacon the ladies fixed in the cook shack.

Rebecca sat at his side, where he wanted to keep her always. She sighed. "I don't think I'll be able to eat again until tomorrow."

Although he'd laughed, he, too, couldn't eat as much as he used to, nor did he need to do so.

Cool, rain-cleared air met them as they departed the cook shack. "Smells fresh, but also muddy." He pointed to the mucky circle where they'd danced the previous night.

Tom shrugged. "At least the showers didn't start till we were all asleep."

Beside Garrett, his future wife groaned. "Some of you may have slept…"

"You can use my shoulder as a pillow." Garrett brushed his lips against her forehead. "Let's load up."

Jo, who'd eaten in the kitchen, ran up from behind them, whipping her apron off. "Let me get my bag and I'll be ready to go."

Their father emerged from the cabin. For once, Pa had allowed himself the luxury of sleeping in. In a few long strides, he joined them. "I'm expectin' a passel of weddings before too long, so let's see you all keep the brides and grooms and the dates straight."

Drawing Rebecca close, Garrett hoped for sooner, rather than later, for a wedding.

Within the half hour, they'd said their goodbyes. Amy ran across the clearing, clutching a cloth doll to her chest. "My grandma says I can go with you!"

She threw her thin arms around Rebecca's middle then stepped back and displayed her doll, with yellow yarn braids that matched Amy's own plaits. "Look what Grandma Pearl made."

CR80

Rebecca instinctively brushed back a strand of golden hair that had fallen into the girl's eyes. "She's almost as pretty as you."

Pink, like a sunset over Lake Michigan, washed the girl's cheeks and she dug the toe of her short boots into the dirt of the hard-packed clearing.

Frenchie directed the horses toward them, then brought them to a halt and secured the large wagon. While it wasn't as old as the dray, the wood was similarly grayed with age. The bed featured four rows of benches behind the driver—enough seating for twelve adults—and a small open section behind, for belongings.

"Mademoiselle Amy, come up front with your grand-père."

The child squealed in delight. Then, as Garrett lifted her skyward, she chortled.

"I reckon I could get used to such a happy sound." Garrett twirled her around, as he'd done with Rebecca the previous day, and joy such as she'd never known planted itself firmly in her heart. This man would be a good husband and father, would make a home with her. Somehow, if they could only settle the differences of where they might live and have their livelihoods.

Frenchie loaded their belongings into the back as Garrett swung Amelia up onto the front seat. One of the horses swished a fly away with his tail but otherwise, the two horses stood steady as Tom offered first Jo and then Rebecca a hand up into the wagon. The engaged couple took the second bench back as Rebecca settled her full skirts around her on the wide plank row behind Amelia, who gleefully occupied a third of the front driver's seat.

"Come on, Grandpa, I want you to show me how to drive."

"I rarely use this vehicle, Mademoiselle Amy," Frenchie carefully sounded out his words, which were hard to understand, with him missing so many teeth. He mounted up and joined Amelia. "I'll need to keep control of this bulky contraption, but I'll let you help a little."

They turned to wave goodbye as Frenchie released the brake and flicked the reins. Within two miles, it was clear why the dray was normally used. Rebecca lifted the watch face from her gold-plated chatelaine. At this pace, they'd be late.

Garrett leaned in, his wool-covered arm pressing into her side and whispered, "We'll get there in time for the boat schedule." When he covered her hand with his, she relaxed, as much as she could, onto the bench seat.

Her sweetheart tapped the driver's shoulder. "I reckon the ladies won't mind if you push those two a little harder. Might rock the wagon more, but Tom and I can keep our ladies steady."

The Frenchman crowed in laughter. As he whistled to the horses, Amelia swiveled to watch as Garrett wrapped an arm around Rebecca and drew her close. The child made a knowing face, her eyes half-closed, and then turned to the front again. Garrett laughed and pressed a kiss to Rebecca's cheek, warming her down to her half-boots.

Rebecca gestured to the massive white pines bordering the heavily rutted road. "I wonder if we'll lose all these beautiful pines."

Frenchie adjusted the reins and directed the team of horses around a water-filled hole in the road. Amelia squealed and clutched his arm.

Rebecca thought she might come out of her seat, but her sweetheart held her fast.

CRISO

Rebecca jostled further into Garrett's arms. He didn't mind, in fact, he rather liked her warm body snug up against his. When she caught him staring overlong at her, twin circles of red appeared on her cheeks.

"I hardly slept last night. It was kind of the cook to let me stay with her in her cabin. But between Irma's snoring, the sounds of the insects in the woods, and my concerns about the mercantile, I don't think I slept more than an hour."

He whispered, "Are you sure you weren't just thinking about me and my kiss?"

"Garrett Christy! I am shocked at you." Her throaty laugh reassured him she wasn't surprised where his thoughts were.

Frenchie groaned as the horses resisted his directions. Finally, he got them going again. "My pardons."

"Just get us back to town and we'll be happy, Frenchie," Jo called out.

They hit the edge of the deep rut and Garrett caught Rebecca in his arms before she bounced off the bench. "Gotcha, sweetheart."

"I've got you." Her teasing tone and dancing hazel eyes gleamed with good humor.

Behind them, Jo and Tom's soft murmurings and laughs reflected the humor that fueled their relationship. Rebecca and he weren't as quick-witted and funny as his sister and her fiancé, but that was fine—God made folks all different for His own good reasons. And Jo had been spared the trials that poor Rebecca had suffered. As they rode on, Rebecca nodded off, her head rested on his shoulder. She must be exhausted. Garrett prayed for her, and for their future, as the wagon rolled on.

Soon they'd arrived in Mackinaw City and said their farewells to Frenchie and his new granddaughter. Then the foursome had boarded the half-full boat and found a secluded spot, with port windows offering glimpses of the water.

Rebecca pointed to the padded benches. "Finally, some comfort! I hate to complain, but those cushions look heavenly to me after the wagon ride."

"I reckon you're a wee bit spoiled by the comforts of being a store owner."

When her mouth widened and eyes narrowed, he wished he'd kept his words to himself.

Jo snorted. "I agree with Rebecca, and I'm a lumber camp boss's daughter, as you well know."

Stroking his chin, Tom slid in beside Jo and sighed in pleasure. "Oh, my, yes, much better for my aching backside."

"Tom!" Jo swatted at his leg. "Mind your manners or we ladies won't sit by you."

"Speak for yourself, sister." Garrett took his spot. "I'm not moving anywhere, and I'd wager two bits that neither is Tom."

Rebecca arched an eyebrow. "First, we hear of Tom's body parts, and now of your gambling schemes?"

He shrugged. "If Amy was with us, she'd spend the entire time telling us all about her new dollies, books, and grandparents." That might be their life soon.

"I wouldn't mind." Rebecca cocked her head at him, her hat sliding sideways.

He pressed the fancy cap back down as she straightened, her fingers brushing his as she located and pulled a pin from the bottom, where dark ribbon edged the straw. "Would you like me to help put that back in?"

"No, I've got it." With a deft movement, she'd resecured the hat.

"Wonder if Amy would like a new hat like that one—a little smaller maybe. And one for Pearl."

"I'm sure she would. Amelia gave her new Easter hat to another child at the orphanage, when she learned her friend had nothing new."

"She's a sweet girl." And Garrett would no doubt have some say in helping the child as she matured. "Did you know my brother, Richard, sent over new gloves for all of the children after that?"

"Yes, the Labrons told me at a community meeting. I really like that couple, competition or not."

"They had the white gloves in stock, and gave him a nice discount." This wasn't exactly where he wanted to head this conversation. It was like going halfway around the hill when he should have stopped at the bottom. "Like me, he has a soft spot for children." He blinked back some mist that must have pressed through the ferry windows. Misty Fawn's children could have been his. But they'd never gotten a chance to grow up. He had to trust God, though, who'd received them into His kingdom. But now, he had another chance to help Frenchie and Pearl with Amy and her siblings.

He had to get Rebecca thinking about coming to the island. Surely she could set up shop there. But he'd not spied a "For Rent" sign anywhere. He should have looked. Should have thought of that. But he hadn't.

She gazed up at him, a honeyed curl bouncing against her lacy bodice as the ship carried them over the frothy waves. "I like children, too."

"Good." He grinned. "I knew that from how you are with Amy."

"And I'd like to help the Brevorts any way I can."

"Me, too. But first I've got to get settled in my new work."

She pressed her pink lips tightly together.

Garrett pointed through the window, to the Grand Hotel, as the steamboat puffed past the island. "Are you familiar with the street that runs next to the hotel?"

"I've been over a few times, but yes, I think I recollect." Rebecca squinted through the portal with him. Haze hung over the water beyond.

"That's where the housing for the craftsmen is. About a half mile down that road. Nice building—clean, neat, and new."

Jo cleared her throat. "And room enough for two?"

"And hopefully more." Garrett ran a hand along Rebecca's smooth jawline.

Tom chuckled. "Like me and Jo, right? We'd love to come visit you."

His sister kicked the toe of Tom's boot. "I don't think my brother meant us."

"Nope." Garrett winked at Rebecca.

Jo scowled at him. "Will you stay all winter?"

"Reckon so. That's the condition of my employment."

Rebecca squeezed his hand as though warning him. "Things aren't exactly settled yet."

After that comment, the foursome sat quietly.

Before long, St. Ignace's shoreline came into view. The nearer they got to the dock, the stronger the odor of smoke grew. Not the familiar scent of hearth fire but a metallic, full ashy stench that assaulted his nostrils.

Tom pointed. "There's a fire!"

⋘⋙

Rebecca clutched at her neck and the cameo she'd pinned there earlier, a gift from her parents many years ago. She pressed Garrett's brawny arm. "I'm afraid."

A muscle in his jaw twitched. Her heartbeat ratcheted upward. He was anxious, too.

Be anxious for nothing.

Jo pressed her face toward the window. "I can't tell where it's coming from."

Oh, God, please don't let it be my store.

Immediately, God convicted her spirit—the safety of those people near the burning property was of more importance. *Please let all be well.*

"Let's go above deck and see." Garrett took her hand and pulled her upward.

The foursome mounted the steps to the main deck and found room to stand at the rail, where the other passengers gawked at the village. The ship bobbed through the waves, onward, into thicker smoke. Jo plucked a handkerchief from her reticule and pressed it to her nose.

Rebecca closed her eyes as Garrett pulled her against the safety of his chest. "Please tell me when you can see where the fire emanates from."

Patting her back at first, soon he shifted to slow stroking motions from her tense neck to the tight muscles in the middle of her corseted back. "Don't look, darlin'," he crooned and then exhaled so deeply that her face pressed into his shirt buttons.

Tom coughed. "Water wagons and sand everywhere." Tom's voice held relief, though.

She pulled away, suddenly aware that Mrs. Jeffries' inn might be afire. But the inn stood tall and proud at the mouth of Moran Bay harbor. Her little shop, or rather what was left of it, wasn't as fortunate.

Rebecca stared in abject horror.

A gap stood between her business and the two adjacent buildings. *Gone.* Ashes. Ashes to ashes, dust to dust. What had once been her escape was gone.

Garrett groaned.

"It's gone," was all she could mutter.

Tom wrapped an arm around Jo. "The fire brigade must have gotten there quickly to have kept that blaze from spreading."

"Thank God." Rebecca tried to be grateful, but fear overwhelmed her and she shook from head to foot. "At least no one was inside."

Leaning over the boat railing, her auburn hair blowing in the breeze, Jo pointed. "Look!"

Tom pulled her back.

"I see Moose, and he's with some tiny lady right near the shop."

Rebecca squinted as the boat sliced through the water, heading for the dock. "The librarian, I believe."

Garrett kissed her forehead. "Juliana and Moose will tell us what happened."

"Yes." Her voice emerged as the barest of whispers.

Docking was a slow, interminable affair, and Rebecca could do nothing but stare with horror at the ruins of her store.

"It'll be all right." Garrett pulled her close. And somehow, with him next to her, she was sure all would be well.

"Yes," she murmured and wiped tears from her eyes.

"Listen, when we get off I want you to let me handle this." He rubbed a sore spot between her shoulder blades. "I got a bad feeling that Peevey might be involved. And if he's anywhere around, I don't want him near you."

A cold chill shot through her as the boat bumped against the dock. Passengers moved toward where the gangplank would allow them to exit, once it was set in place.

Jo's lilac scent carried as she leaned in and kissed Rebecca's cheek. "There's always hope, my future sister. If I've learned anything in this life, it's to never give up. Believe that God will help."

Garrett released her. "My only hope is in God, not my fists anymore. But I'm prepared to keep Rebecca safe if her attacker caused this fire."

Shaking, Rebecca clung to his hand as Jo placed her arm around her. Her legs went weak.

On shore, a nun waved at them—Sister Mary Lou, gripping a large black pouch in her other hand.

As they hurried to disembark, Rebecca spotted Mrs. Jeffries and Charlie in the crowd. Tom turned to Jo as they stepped onto the dock. "Let me run to my mother and see what she knows."

The ash and smoke in the air caused most people to fish for handkerchiefs and cover their noses. Rebecca and Jo began to cough. A light breeze stirred and as they moved down the walkway, the odor began to dissipate inland. Wisps of smoke clung to the tall pines that hugged the shoreline beyond town.

ᏣᏍᎣ

Certain that Rebecca would remain behind his back, and protected, Garrett crossed the street with her trailing him. A deputy was speaking with the librarian and Moose, who sported the beginnings of a shiner on his left eye. *What in tarnation?*

"Hello, sir, this is Miss Hart, the proprietress of the store." Garrett gestured to Rebecca and then offered his hand.

The deputy didn't shake his hand. Instead, he nodded at Rebecca. "Good thing you weren't here, miss."

Seated on a nearby bench, Juliana was covered in ash and her hands were red, possibly burned.

Rebecca went to the young woman. "You need to get your hands into cold water right away."

"Don't be rubbing butter in those burns," Garrett cautioned. Ma said such advice was the worst thing she'd seen for kitchen accidents. She always had her ladies press their hands into cool water.

"We won't," Rebecca called over her shoulder.

The librarian sobbed as Rebecca wrapped an arm around her waist and escorted her down the street to the barber shop, where there was sure to be plentiful water.

"I'm Deputy Williams." The officer pointed a stout finger at him. "Who are you, sir?"

"Garrett Christy."

When the man quirked an eyebrow, Garrett added, "I'm Miss Hart's fiancé."

"I see. Well, your fiancée is fortunate she wasn't here or she'd likely be dead."

"Was it Myron Peevey?"

After removing his hat, the sheriff's deputy tucked it under his arm. "Don't know the man's name…"

Moose strode over. "It was Peevey all right. He was in there waiting for Janie to come back."

"Janie?" Deputy Williams scratched his chin.

"Miss Hart, that is Daggenhart—her full name is Rebecca Jane Daggenhart, soon to be Mrs. Garrett Christy." Garrett's mouth seemed to have acquired a steam-generated motor. "And Peevey tried to kill her downstate ten years back. Me and my brother, Richard here, saved her from drowning."

The officer's dark eyebrows pulled into one long line. "Slow down."

Moose passed a singed piece of rope to the policeman. "He tried to hang her a long time ago, officer. And he failed. I think he was planning on trying it, again."

Clenching his fists, Garrett wished he could strangle Peevey. If only the judge and the court hadn't been controlled by the lumberman who the wretch worked for—then Peevey may have hung, or been kept in prison far longer.

Firemen opened the mercantile's doors, releasing an awful stench. All pressed wet rags to their faces. After a few minutes passed, they emerged empty-handed.

The tallest fireman joined the deputy. "We think we got it all out, but we're not moving the body."

"He's dead?" Moose's Adam's apple bobbed.

"Peevey?" Was Garrett wrong to wish it so?

∞

"Thank God you weren't here, Rebecca." Juliana groaned as she continued to plunge her hands into the cold-water bath.

"Yes, indeed, and I wish you hadn't been." Rebecca turned toward the barber. "Do you have any salve, Pete?"

Mr. Anderson brought a small ceramic jar of pungent ointment to them, and Rebecca dried her friend's hands with a fresh cotton towel and covered them with ointment. "I don't think you'll need gauze unless they blister."

"The brass doorknob was hot by the time I was able to get past that horrible man." Juliana's eyes widened. "I think he was looking for you. Kept saying he wanted the store owner, and I wasn't Janie."

Her stomach threatened to heave its contents at the thought. God had kept her away.

You obeyed.

But she hadn't wanted her friend to be hurt.

Juliana winced in pain. "I thought he was insane."

"Because he is. Or was." Rebecca dried her hands and tried not to inhale the overpowering odor of the ointment. "What on earth were you doing in the store?"

Juliana's cheeks began to match her hands in redness. "I'm so ashamed. I wanted to see if Sister Mary Lou had brought my dress back for the dance."

Of course, the librarian could not possibly have suspected Peevey would be in there, but to think Juliana could have lost her life over a dress… Rebecca closed her eyes. *Thank you, Lord, for keeping my friend safe.*

"I borrowed the key for the shop and went in. But I smelled something strong—like a lamp had spilled. So I quickly opened the armoire to see if my dress was hanging in there but it was empty—"

"Empty?" Sister Mary Lou was to have placed them all there …

"Yes, and I was so disappointed and I wasn't paying attention until I heard this whoosh sound and heard and smelled smoke and fire."

"Oh my." Rebecca pressed her hands to her stomach.

"This man came flying at me from the back room and I stared at him. He clutched a hank of rope and looked like a madman." Juliana shuddered. "He stopped and said, 'You're not Janie.'"

"He meant me—I used to go by that name as a child." Rebecca's shivers returned.

"Heavens, he meant to kill you." Juliana blinked back tears. "*No*, was all I could utter and then he began to scream, as though the hounds of hell had found him."

"Oh merciful Father." Rebecca sank onto the stool adjacent to her friend.

"Exactly. So I'm staring like a ninny as these balls of fire are coming at us and then the door opens and Mr. Christy rushes in and knocks the man to the floor and…" Tears poured down her friend's cheeks.

"What happened?"

"That lunatic punched him in the eye and Richard punched him back. Then Richard tossed me over his shoulder and carried me out of there like I was a sack of potatoes!"

Mr. Anderson drew closer. "Providence, Miss Juliana, God's watching over you both today."

She nodded. "After we got out, we heard that overhead beam fall."

Was Peevey dead? Was she wrong to wish it?

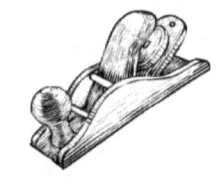

Chapter Sixteen

They all assembled in the inn's parlor, which had been decorated in shades of cream, pink, and green—not exactly Garrett's favorite colors.

Moose hadn't spoken since he'd returned from the lumber camp with the sheriff. And now, seated there with them, Garrett's younger brother determinedly twisted, pulled, and crushed his red cap until Jo finally went over to him and snatched it away.

"Stop that or I'll get my spoon out!"

Garrett laughed. Leave it to his sister to break the tension in the room.

Sheriff Edwards raised both hands, palms up. "I brought you together to review some facts before I send in my report. First off, I want you to all know I am glad for your cooperation. By working together, we know that the two recent deaths in the county were murders, not natural deaths. And we're sure Peevey had motivation and did the killing."

Jo clasped her hands. "So, he killed that poor lumberjack living in the shack by the new camp?"

"Yes, ma'am, Peevey buried that fellow in the woods nearby."

"Someone needs to notify his wife," Moose muttered. The bruising around his eye, was building toward a spectacular shiner. But thank God his baby brother was otherwise unharmed.

His sister shuddered and moved to Tom's side. "Let's sit down."

The two occupied the loveseat.

Rebecca poured herself a cup of tea from the sideboard, her hands shaking. "And the locksmith, too?"

Crooking a finger at his beloved, Garrett patted the seat beside him with his other hand and she joined him.

"That's right, miss. The doctor thought the marks on his body were mighty odd, but with him being elderly, he'd not thought overmuch about it. But from Peevey's debris at the shack, we've found keys to about half the businesses in town, including your mercantile. We believe there was a struggle, and Peevey killed the locksmith, then made it look as though he'd died in his sleep."

Garrett rubbed his bristly chin, which was in bad need of a shave. He'd not taken Pa's suggestion to stop at the barber's for a shave, and there had been no time since. "So he thought he'd kill Rebecca and burn her mercantile down, too?"

He felt a shudder pass through her and took hold of her hand.

Sheriff Edwards slacked his hip. "He had a small sloop rented in the harbor, so apparently he thought he'd get away on that."

Cordelia paled. "He must have been waiting there in the back, expecting Miss Hart."

"Yes, ma'am. From Deputy Williams's report and my own investigation, that appears so." The Sheriff's gaze touched on each of them. "Hard to believe one man could do so much harm so quickly, and him just out of prison."

"Thank God that Rebecca wasn't here." Garrett squeezed her palm.

"Yes." She sighed and he leaned in to kiss her soft cheek. "I'm so sorry Juliana suffered those burns because of me, though."

"Miss Beauchamps had to work or she'd be here, Sheriff." A strange expression passed over Moose's face, one Garrett couldn't quite decipher. Could it be his little brother had feelings for the librarian?

"Yes, she sent me a note." The sheriff cleared his throat. "According to the prison warden, the deceased Mr. Peevey had no surviving kin."

"No. His mother died when he was very young and his father was killed just before…"

Garrett interrupted, "Before he tried to murder Janie, I mean Rebecca Jane here."

"Can't believe he's finally gotten his due." Moose narrowed his eyes. "Nor can I reckon how someone could end up so evil."

Sheriff Edward shook his head. "I heard you two men rescued her from the AuSable. It was in the records they sent up. Seems like God must have wanted these two brothers to keep you safe, Miss Daggenhart."

Blinking up at Garrett, through tear-filled eyes, Rebecca smiled broadly—like she did when she was young. "Yes, I'd agree."

Although he was mightily tempted to kiss her full on the lips right then and there, Garrett resisted.

Later.

CS🙰

Two days since the fire and the terse telegram from her father left no doubt that Herschel Daggenhart valued money over his only daughter's life. A dull ache settled in her chest as she reread the note. Rebecca handed it to

Garrett to read and she slumped down into a mauve moiré satin chair in the inn's parlor.

"I can't believe any Christian man would send this message to anyone, much less his daughter, after what just happened."

"My father's bottom line was what this fire was going to cost him."

Garrett tapped the message against his thigh. "My pa was right about him—I hate to say it."

"Nothing so bracing as getting your worst fears about a person confirmed." Rebecca motioned for him to sit next to her.

He remained standing. "Makes me want to go down there and give that man a piece of my mind. Or a taste of my fists, if he wasn't your father."

"Now, now." She couldn't help smiling, though, at Garrett's desire to protect her and fight for her.

The doorman knocked on the parlor door before sliding the pocket doors open. "Sister Mary Lou to see you."

"Oh, please send her in." Rebecca rose as the nun entered the room.

Garrett squeezed Rebecca's shoulder as he left and smiled at their friend. "Sister, good to see you."

She nodded back at him as he slipped out, pulling the paneled doors closed. Absent her usual entourage of orphans, Sister Mary Lou came to Rebecca and pulled her into a quick embrace and kissed her on the cheek, wafting the scent of incense mixed with violets.

"Please, have a seat." Rebecca pointed to the floral divan.

"Thank you, I think I will." Pulling her habit's skirts forward, she appeared to collapse onto the couch. "I wanted to tell you, in person, how very sorry I am about what happened."

"Thank you." Rebecca sighed in relief. "I'm so grateful Juliana and Richard were spared. I'm so sorry that even at the end, Peevey wouldn't give up his evil quest and perished because of it."

"God gives us free will, my dear." She slipped her hands into the folds of her black garment.

The grandfather clock behind them chimed the hour.

"I don't have a lot of time to chat. But I wanted to tell you that I have all of the dresses back at the convent."

"You do? Thank God. I thought you must because of what Juliana said, but I wasn't sure."

"Yes, I do…but Father Paul is insisting that I move them out—I'd told him, as I promised you, that they'd be gone days ago."

"I see but, again, thank divine Providence they weren't returned." How terrible that would have been for her and for the community.

"Yes." A smile brightened her solemn face. "And the young ladies who'll attend the Lumberjacks' Ball will be relieved."

"Yes. And maybe the men?"

She laughed. "I think our librarian, especially."

"According to Garrett, his brother has finally gotten the sense to invite her. That's the one good thing that has come from this awful event."

A smile tugged at the nun's lips. "I wouldn't count on that being the only blessing God shall bring from this evil." She pulled a black pouch from the voluminous folds of her black habit. "I have a third of the money here for the fabric and notions for the fund raiser. People who knew about the loan were anxious to help out by purchasing ahead."

Rebecca rubbed the back of her neck, easing some of the tension there. With the money from the dresses, Rebecca could recoup some of her losses, too. She'd need to reimburse Sister Mary Lou for her labor or credit the work against her bill.

"I fully intend to compensate you for the rest of our loan."

"Thank you, Sister Mary Lou. My father will be relieved."

"Your father must be counting his blessings that you were unharmed."

Did he? Had her father ever been grateful she'd been spared? Had he ever taken into account what she enjoyed or wished to do with her life?

Cordelia Jeffries popped her head in the doorway. "Tea time."

Warmth coursed through Rebecca. "I love tea time."

The inn owner arched an eyebrow at her. "I know you do, dear— something we need to discuss."

What did that mean? Just because Rebecca enjoyed preparing the sandwiches and selecting the tea assortment? Perhaps she'd overstepped her bounds, but she took such comfort in a tea done well.

"Yes, ma'am." She hoped her contrite tone extended her apologies, but Mrs. Jeffries' features twitched in confusion.

"We'll be pouring in here momentarily and I'd love to have your help, dear."

"Oh, yes, certainly…" Rebecca hopped up, eager to assist.

"Father Paul will have me saying extra penance if I don't get back soon." Sister Mary Lou stood.

Mrs. Jeffries smiled. "Good to see you, Sister."

"Yes, indeed," Rebecca echoed.

The nun squared her shoulders. "Mrs. Jeffries…I have a favor to ask."

The inn owner's lower lip drew in. "How can I help?"

"I have a dozen gowns that Father Paul wants out of the building by tomorrow, and I'd heard your upper floor may be vacant."

"Afraid so." She shrugged. "And, yes, you could bring them here to the hotel."

A Cheshire Cat grin tugged at Sister Mary Lou's lips. "I believe I know a way we could also get those rooms rented — at least temporarily."

"Do tell." Mrs. Jeffries playfully cupped a hand around her ear. "I'm all ears."

Sister Mary Lou laughed. "How about I come for tea time tomorrow? That's my free day."

"Certainly." The inn owner followed the nun out into the entryway.

As Sister Mary Lou exited, Rebecca overheard Charlie's voice, at the door. In a minute, the porter from the docks rapped at the half-open pocket door. "Miss Hart?"

"Yes?"

The elderly man shifted back and forth, his hat clutched in his hands. "What're we supposed to do about your boxes?"

"Boxes?"

His wrinkled cheeks flushed red. "The ones I kept at the wharf."

Why did he look so guilty?

"Oh! I'd almost forgotten." Another burst of relief caused her to feel almost dizzy. "The shipments you've been holding for me, since I left."

"Yes, miss."

"How many do you have?" They could stack five or six crates in her room.

Head bowed, silver hair glistening beneath the gas lamps, he sighed. "That's the thing, Miss Hart. I'm afeared I haven't been keepin' up with yer deliveries. I was tryin' my durnedest to tell you at the wharf the other day."

"Oh?"

"I've had a real bad bout of rheumatism with the last rain. And, well, I left 'em in storage but now they got to go."

"I see."

"My boss says he needs them off the dock by this afternoon."

"How many crates? What kind of weight?" No wonder shipments had slowed. Rebecca tried to recall her last orders. "What is in them?"

"The thing is, all this fancy stuff, these breakables—they're lightweight but there's plenty of 'em. I wasn't real sure I could manage the lot of 'em without breakage."

"Oh. I think I know." She exhaled. "Sample china tea cups and saucers from vendors throughout the East coast, is my guess."

Charlie nodded. "That's some of 'em, miss, I believe from the markings on the crates. But the rest is things people in these parts consider frivolities—although the summer clientele might appreciate the finery, but they ain't here yet for the season. There's honey, tea, packaged crackers, and cookies."

"I see." Which meant there also may be silver-plated teaspoons. The pretty things in life that she enjoyed. What else had she sent for? Father had said these items wouldn't sell.

"Sorry about your loss, Miss Hart." The deliveryman dipped his chin. "Guess I shoulda said that first, eh?"

Stifling a chuckle, she shook her head. "It's all right. Life goes on."

"It certainly does." Mrs. Jeffries swept in with a tray of ham biscuits. She offered some to Charlie.

"Thanks, Mrs. Jeffries." The porter took two big bites.

The inn proprietress cocked her head. "Do you think the lumberjacks and their ladies might enjoy these for their dance?"

"Mmm, yes, ma'am."

She offered him another and he accepted, grinning.

Garrett entered the room, humming. He swiped two biscuits from the tray and winked at Mrs. Jeffries. "I heard your question as I was coming in and think I should be the judge of that."

Rebecca plucked one of the warm biscuits from his hand. "Charlie was telling me about some crates I have at the wharf."

"They need movin'?" Garrett said around a mouthful of biscuit. He wiped crumbs from his face.

"Sure do, but can't do it by myself."

"Me and my brother could help you."

Charlie quirked an eyebrow upward. "Today?"

"Let me go get him." Garrett grabbed two more biscuits. "Right after I'm done sampling these."

The dockworker inclined his head toward the inn's owner. "Say, Mrs. Jeffries, have you got room somewhere in this big place for about ten dollies worth of goods?"

Rebecca gasped. "Those can't all be mine. You mean four big boxes each load?"

"Yes, miss. Could take me and the Christy men over two hours to get them here unless I can locate a dray."

"Take our wagon." Mrs. Jeffries set the tray down on a side table. "No one is using it."

"Thank you so much." Rebecca smiled at her landlady, who was a real gem.

"Appreciate it, Cordelia." Garrett leaned over Rebecca and took yet another biscuit and handed another to Charlie, who grinned.

Mrs. Jeffries feigned disgust at the men. "And if Garrett has room in the workshop out back, I think that would be the perfect place to store your merchandise, Rebecca."

In two weeks, Garrett would be moved to the island. What was she to do?

"Why don't I send my men to help you, Charlie, while Garrett readies his workshop?" Mrs. Jeffries removed the tray from the table again and headed toward the back.

Forty crates of goods? And no shop in which to sell them.

"Come on back, Rebecca." Mrs. Jeffries called over her shoulder. "Don't forget we still have tea time to prepare for today."

CSWO

With a quarter of his best tools gone, destroyed in the fire, what was Garrett going to do? His job on the island was contingent upon him bringing his own woodworking implements. He scanned the workshop and began sorting out what he had left.

An hour later, sweating, he'd ventured back into the inn looking for lemonade. Instead, he'd heard the patrons laughing in the parlor, where no doubt they were enjoying tea and all the pretty little treats Rebecca and Cordelia conjured up. Not fit for a man but the ladies sure relished them— tomato aspic, coconut cookies too tiny for a man's fingers, miniature bowls of rice salad, Madelines, and shortbread cookies imprinted with designs so fancy it seemed a shame to eat them, and more. Give him a big ham biscuit and lemonade any day and he'd be happy.

Foraging, he located the pitcher of lemonade on the servants' table in the back of the big kitchen. He poured himself a mason jar full and tossed back the contents. *Lord, I've slaked my thirst, but I need some help, elsewise this is gonna be one long afternoon and I need to get to the bank.*

The back door swung in. Moose stood framed there, the top of his head almost hitting the jamb. "Thought I'd find you in here."

"How are you, brother?"

Moose held out his hairy hand and wobbled it. "Fair to middlin', if you must know."

"Why's that?" Garrett was the one who had lost the tools of his trade.

"Pa's coming over here to check out the new camp, and he sent a message that I had to hire a passel of cooks. Do you know why?"

"Uh, well first off there's Jo, which you already knew about. She's not cooking."

"Yup."

"And Pearl plans to come to the island?"

Moose's jaw dropped open. "You got yerself yer own cook?"

Garrett held both palms up to his brother. "Nope. She's got her grandkids to care for now."

"Grandkids?"

"Yup. That little Amy that trailed after Rebecca is one of 'em."

"You're joshing me."

"Nope. And there were several more at the orphanage on the island. So I brought 'em to their grandma and new grandpa."

"Whooee, I can't picture Frenchie with a slew of grandkids. And those two are long in the tooth for this new job."

Moose's words echoed those convicting his heart that he should do something. "I plan to help when I'm not working." And he hoped Rebecca would accept his proposal of marriage and feel led to aid him, maybe the two even taking over the raising of the kids if need be. A ready-made family, but an awfully sweet one.

"Well, that's two cooks, but who is the third one?"

"Dunno." He scratched his head.

"Well, Pa should be here soon, and he can tell us."

"Pa's coming?"

"Yup."

"Wait, I remember now—Ruth isn't gonna cook anymore."

"Figures." Richard shoved his hands into his dungarees and rocked back and forth, his eyes lighting on each set of tools. "Looks like you got most of your stuff. I thought Pa was coming to help get you back on your feet."

Heat steamed his face. "I'm a man and I'll take care of my own losses, thank you very much."

"Seems to me that Daggenhart should reimburse you…"

"I'll never ask for a red cent from that man." He made fists then flexed his fingers open again. Daggenhart could end up being his father-in-law.

"All right, all right, don't get angry at me."

"Sit down for a spell and have some lemonade—it's good."

"Can't. I'm going to the docks to watch for Pa."

"I'd join you, but I need to go down to the bank." For a loan. And to withdraw what he'd already deposited there.

Chapter Seventeen

Y ou're so good at entertaining, you should consider doing this for a living." Cordelia smiled at Rebecca as the two removed the remnants of their afternoon tea from the parlor.

The sunshine, filtering through the lace curtains, illuminated a few dust motes. "I don't think hosting tea parties is something one does as a business." At least not one that would bring in the type of income a mercantile could.

"If my sister weren't coming to take over the catering and tea parties here at the inn, I'd offer you the job—you enjoy this so much."

"Really? She's going to run a Tea House here?" Maybe there was a possibility somewhere. Rebecca straightened and smiled. "I do love it! From finding the perfect cups and saucers to the prettiest napkins and linens. It's a pleasure to me. But as a business…"

"Delivery, Miss Hart." The doorman called through the half open door.

"Must be Charlie." Rebecca followed Cordelia down the hallway, each carrying stacks of dishes, which they placed on the empty kitchen table. Their young dish washer should be there shortly.

"Go ahead and show them how you want those crates, Rebecca, and I'll finish up."

"Thanks." Wiping her hands, she exited through the back door, hurried down the steps, and then strode to the workshop.

The drayman and Mrs. Jeffries' assistants rolled chest-high stacked crates on dollies into the workshop. As she approached, she spied *TEA, COFFEE, HONEY, SPICES* etched on the wooden slates in black block lettering. Maybe the inn's owner would offer to buy some of the supplies. Or Rebecca could check with the restaurants.

One after another, the men rolled in dollies piled with boxes. Rebecca shook her head, trying to recall what all she'd ordered. Had she erred in recording the figures when she ordered?

"This bunch is a whole lot lighter than that was." Charlie pushed a cart in with boxes marked *CHINA*, *samples*, and *various suppliers*. "But it also says frah-jilly."

Rebecca frowned, not understanding. Then she saw *FRAGILE* marked on the side. At least he could read. *Sort of.* That was something. As long as he knew what it meant.

He removed his wool cap and wiped his forehead. "So I was extra careful with these. Although frah-jilly stuff isn't something you commonly see around here, eh?"

When they finished, she paid them, adding a tip from the purse Sister Mary Lou had left for her. She faced the crates, also realizing she needed to face facts. She really wasn't a great businesswoman. She'd ordered what caught her fancy. Familiar shame tried to gain hold in her spirit, but she resisted. Her parents had shamed her the past decade. God wouldn't do that to her, nor would she visit the horrid feeling upon herself again.

"What all have you got here?" Mrs. Jeffries stood, arms akimbo, in the doorway.

"We should check and see." Hopefully, the inn could benefit from some of these purchases. The two of them began opening each crate.

Cordelia Jeffries pulled a rose and lilac teacup from a straw-filled container. "This is fabulous." She held it aloft, sunshine streaming through the side windows meeting where she stood.

"And free!" Rebecca laughed. "The vendors must have all shipped me their samples within days of each other because all seven of those crates are marked as China. I'm betting the boxes hold teacups and saucers. All orphan sets now."

What a pity that no one in the area would be ordering the lovely designs.

The innkeeper frowned. "Are they all similar to this one?"

Rebecca retrieved a violet and daisy chintz boneware teacup. "Yes, and so beautiful."

"And so expensive." The woman's low voice chided.

Slumping to the floor, Rebecca looked up. "I don't know what I was thinking."

"People in these parts aren't likely to order such fancy patterns. A few, maybe, but the summer folks tend to bring theirs up with them from down state. But at least you aren't out any money for them." She moved to another box and using a small crowbar pried free the slats. She unrolled the wrapping around an odd-shaped item and held it aloft. "Teapots? There must be four porcelain teapots in this box. And they gave them to you?"

No. She'd foolishly ordered them when she'd learned they weren't free. "Afraid not."

"If I didn't already have sufficient supplies I'd buy these from you…"

Rebecca raised her hand to stop her. "It's not your fault." It was no one's fault that a madman had befriended her as a child and later tried to kill her. Not once, but twice. Yet here she was.

A pucker formed between Cordelia's eyebrows. "I don't know why God saved you, child."

Prickles went down Rebecca's arms. It was as if the woman read her mind. Or as if the Holy Spirit spoke to both of them.

"But I believe you are here for a purpose." She pressed a hand to Rebecca's shoulder. "Life is short, my dear. I've learned you need to do what you love. God puts that joy in your heart when you are doing what pleases Him. And I've seen that glow of peaceful joy on your face when you're serving tea, preparing goodies, and all that. You love people, that's for sure."

"I do. I'll pray about it."

"Good, and let's see what else you've got here."

"Should be honey in many flavors, teas of all types, coffees…"

She laughed. "Mercy's sake, you've got enough goods there for a tea shop of your own."

A tea shop.

An hour later, Rebecca sat in front of Mr. Jenkins at the Lumbermen's Bank and spewed out her story. Then she waited.

He sat, his fingers steepled in front of him as he leaned on his elbows. His thinning hair covered his bowl shaped head and his gray eyes seemed unfocused, as though he were lost in thought. "Young lady, I cannot help you here."

She bowed her head. At least she'd tried.

He cleared his throat. "But if you are willing to set up shop on Mackinac Island, I believe I have something that could benefit us both."

Mackinac, where Garrett would be going.

Reaching into a cigar box, he paused. "Mind if I smoke?"

She did, but this wasn't her office nor her bank. Instead of answering, she asked, "Can you tell me about what you have in mind?"

After trimming the end and lighting the cigar, he drew in a long puff and slowly exhaled it, thankfully away from her. His twitching lips suggested he was refraining from laughing. Was he mocking her?

"I know of a rental available on the main street in the heart of Mackinac Island's tourist district."

Her heartbeat skittered. She could be near Garrett. And the children. "Yes?"

Mr. Jenkins laughed. "I'm hoping that's what you'll say to my proposition."

She blinked rapidly, not liking the word he'd chosen. "Why is that?"

"You see, my brother-in-law financed the move for the last client, a jeweler, from that prime spot to a newer building closer to the fort."

"You sound troubled, sir—why?"

"I lost my income." He brought his free hand down on his walnut desktop and Rebecca flinched. "But with your business background and the fact that you already have the merchandise and are ready to go, why, I could set you up immediately."

She swallowed. "And your terms? I'd have to discuss that with my fiancé." And she'd have to let Garrett know that he was, indeed, her fiancé. As of one minute ago when she needed to ascertain what sort of man this banker was.

He chuckled. "My wife is going to love this. She and her brother have had a rivalry for years over that store. You see, we own it and we'd purchased it before he'd gotten a chance to. And he's resented that fact ever since."

"I really don't want to get in the middle of a family feud." She had enough family difficulties of her own to last a lifetime.

"No, no, Miss Hart, I think we have a plan that might show him what God can do and what mercy can, also."

Her head began to ache. "How so?"

"You'd wish to eventually purchase the store?"

"Yes, sir. Eventually."

"Good. And I've already met with your future husband earlier. Fine young man."

She stiffened. What had Garrett done?

The banker grabbed his fountain pen and scribbled something on a sheet of paper then handed it to her. "There are four bedrooms upstairs, which I believe would work quite nicely for the children."

The children?

"The old folks might need the downstairs bedroom. It's small but cozy."

The old folks. Did he mean Mr. and Mrs. Brevort?

"The kitchen is also on the lower level, with the store in front. Let me show you a rough diagram."

Jenkins pulled out another sheet and quickly sketched out what appeared to be a deep rectangular building with a first and second story. "There is a balcony up top and a play area behind with enough grass to please most tykes. And it's only a hop, skip, and jump from the boardwalk and beach.

Close enough to the last dock that you could set up an arrangement for them to handle all your deliveries."

He named the square footage and her head began to swim. Mr. Jenkins tapped the page where he'd indicated the monthly rent. "I'll drop that after the season lets off. But the locals will likely keep you in business, too. Velma's family will make sure of that. Velma's my wife and her kin includes some of the seasonal high and mighties like James Reynolds, the steel magnate, and Derik Cross, the lumber baron."

"I don't know what to say."

"Right up front I need to tell you of a condition I have if you choose to buy."

"What's that?"

"You'll have to finance through my brother-in-law's bank on the island, and any loans must first be run through him." Mr. Jenkins drew in on his cigar.

"This is the man who got your tenant to move?"

"Yes, but Velma and I are done playing this game with him. I'm hoping if he sees I'm making an effort then maybe he'll stop. Sending business his way is bound to get his attention."

"But why are you helping me?"

He squashed out his cigar and rose from his desk, moving to a nearby window overlooking the street. "Miss Hart, you would not believe the people who have streamed into this office and out again, wanting me to help you get back on your feet after the fire. I don't think I've seen anything like it. Even Father Paul came in and Sister Mary Lou."

Tears began to form in her eyes and she blinked them back. "But I'm sure you had to tell them that my own father has refused to back me."

Steel gray eyes pierced hers. "That's the thing that got me. Everyone who came in here said you were a wonderful young lady with a good head on your shoulders. Yet your father wished to withdraw your line of credit."

"That reminds me." Rebecca retrieved the bag from her friend, Sister Mary Lou. "I need to leave payment with the teller."

"No need, miss. It's already been taken care of."

"How?"

"A little here and a little there all adds up, doesn't it?"

"You mean…" Tears clogged her throat, preventing her from completing her sentence.

He nodded. "I thought to myself, a businesswoman who can command that kind of loyalty in such a short time deserves a break."

Did he know about Peevey? The grapevine might have already spread the word.

"In any event, although I couldn't see anything here on the mainland, I prayed over it and the answer was right in front of me." Jenkins displayed a For Rent sign that included a picture of the building. "So I'd say your true Father was, and is, watching out for you."

At that, tears overflowed and Rebecca fished a handkerchief from her reticule. "I don't know how I can thank you."

"Just be successful, do what I said, and that will be all the thanks my missus and I could hope for." He tapped his ashes into a brass tray. "She'd love to see her brother again. None of us are getting any younger."

"I'm speechless." She shook her head slowly.

"Why don't you come back with your young man and you can sign the papers?"

"With Garrett?"

"Seeing as he'll eventually be inhabiting the building, too, and owning it with you, I think that's prudent. It's good business, Miss Hart."

Did Garrett see her as good business? Was she substituting another man for her father and his control over her?

She squared her shoulders. "And if Mr. Christy prefers not to co-sign?"

☙❧

Garrett surveyed the stacks of crates and whistled. If Rebecca listened to his plan, what would it cost to transport them to the island store? He turned to his pa and Cordelia. "You reckon her pa will try to come and take all this?"

Cordelia held up several sheets and first showed them to Tom. "I totaled the invoices and she'd have to come up with a fair amount."

Pa took the papers. "I'll pay them myself before we let that little gal ask Daggenhart for a penny. Lousy so-and-so."

"Pa, Daggenhart is my future father-in-law." Garrett dipped his chin.

"Truth is truth, son." He crinkled his nose.

The innkeeper tapped the sides of the crates on the right side of the room. "All of this merchandise was free. Can you believe it?"

"Free?" Tom leaned over one of the open crates, in which lay four teacup sets.

Garrett couldn't fathom it. Who would send out free wares?

"Samples?" Pa made a face. "What could she do with china samples, though?"

Mrs. Lilly joined him, clutching a pitcher of lemonade and a set of nested glasses. "Those cups would be perfect for a tearoom as would the comestibles."

Comestibles?

Tom leaned in. "Food," he whispered.

"Don't think tea, cookies, and crackers qualify as my kind of food." Garrett pried open another box. "Now here's some good stuff. Cherries, apple slices, and peaches."

Rebecca's eyes widened as she entered the workshop. Garrett opened his arms to her as she shot right toward him, tears streaming down her pale cheeks. He pressed his head against her forehead. "What's wrong, love?"

"Nothing." She sniffed and dabbed at her nose with a wadded up handkerchief. He fished his own clean one from his pocket and handed it to her.

She turned to face Mrs. Lilly. "As I was walking back here, I had that same idea—that all those mismatched— but beautiful—teacups and saucers would be perfect for a tearoom."

"How about a tea shop with a tearoom? With enough room upstairs so Pearl and Frenchie and the kids could stay on the island, too?" Garrett leaned away from her to look into her eyes.

They both spoke at the same time, "I've got the place!"

Laughter broke out.

Pa clapped his hands. Cordelia, Moose, and Mrs. Lilly joined in, too.

Pa gestured for the others to follow him out. "Looks like these two got some talking to do."

"Yeah, and they don't need an audience." Tom winked as he took Jo's elbow and escorted her from the room.

Pa called over his shoulder, "All right if that inventory is my wedding present?"

"Yes!" Rebecca and Garrett chorused.

Chapter Eighteen

Mackinac Island

Rebecca pinched herself as she surveyed the new shop situated smack dab in the heart of downtown Mackinac Island.

"You gotta stop doing that or you'll be black and blue before long." Garrett swept an errant curl from her eyes.

"I can't believe how big this place is." She waved her arms overhead "And look how clean."

"I like clean." He leaned in and wrapped his arms around her waist. "Clean is good."

"We've been saved so much work."

"Which means we have more time for this." Garrett nuzzled her neck, tickling her, and she laughed, then pulled away.

"Better hold those thoughts until after we're married, Mr. Christy." But when he drew her closer, again, she didn't protest, only sighed in satisfaction.

Garrett kissed the top of her head. "I will…"

She laughed as he pressed against her and kissed her soundly. "I don't know if I believe you."

Garrett slowly released her and held her at arm's length. "What I can't believe is that you're supposed to open shop tomorrow."

"Believe it! Jo sent her baked goods over, just like she said she would every week." Cookies, pies, cakes, and doughnuts covered the new marble-topped counter. "And I suspect that before long I'll also have learned how to bake some delicious goodies on my own."

"Mr. Doud's market will keep you supplied with most things you need." Garrett scanned the open shelves, filled about halfway. "And we can also bring over other supplies from the mainland except after the Straits freeze over."

"This winter should be interesting but different—since we'll be cut off from the mainland."

"Not if we're together." Garrett grinned. "I'll get to sample your home cooking, too."

"Pearl already has a menu planned for us for tonight." She pressed her hands to her hot cheeks. "And Frenchie found us our own carriage and horses for a steal."

"You might not feel that way when you see the feed bill." He clucked his tongue. "Big horses come with big appetites."

"True, but you have to admit they're beautiful."

"That they are. And Frenchie will have them busy in no time and likely drum up some business for himself."

"Whatever makes him happy." Soon Garrett would make her the happiest woman on earth. And a happier couple than Pearl and Frenchie she'd never seen.

"Rebecca, you've done me the honor of accepting my proposal, but there's one more thing I wish to ask." His handsome features hardened into a serious mask.

"What is it?"

"I think you've forgotten a special event in St. Ignace." He took two steps in, lifted her off her feet and spun her around. "Will you accompany me to the Lumberjacks' Ball?"

When he set her back down on the dark hardwood floor she tapped her toe and frowned. "Will banker Jenkins forgive us for shutting down shop for a few days?"

Garrett closed one eye and squinted at her out of the other. "I think you need to say yes."

"Why?"

"Because Pastor Jones is performing a wedding *right after* the dance, and I'd like us both to attend."

She tried to keep a straight face and not laugh at his audacity. "You can't tell me Richard got Juliana to marry him already."

"Nah, they haven't even had their first date."

They both laughed. "Some men move fast."

"Especially the Christy men." He winked at her. "I tell you what. I'm gonna give you a clue as to who is getting wed."

Jutting out her chin, she gazed into his dark eyes. "What kind of clue?"

"Close your eyes."

She mimicked his earlier one-eyed squint, but he shook his index finger at her.

"No cheating. Both eyes closed."

Closing her eyes, she inhaled the scent of tealeaves, sweet pastries, and Garrett's hair tonic. He lifted her chin with two fingers and then stepped in and wrapped his arms around her. She wasn't afraid as his hands wrapped around her neck and pulled her hairpins free. This man would never harm her. Rebecca relaxed and her lips parted allowing him to deepen the kiss. He groaned as he broke free and then trailed kisses down first one side of her neck and then the other.

She gasped as he unbuttoned her top two mother-of-pearl buttons and pressed a gentle kiss to the scar left there so many years earlier. A scar, a rope burn, that Garrett had healed with his love. Trembling, she clutched his muscular forearms.

He stepped back, reached into his pocket, and drew out a heart-shaped garnet pendant—one his mother had worn into her father's shop when she used to come to town. The delicate rose-gold chain unfolded as he held it out, unclasped it, and then encircled her neck with it. His fingers trembled against her neck as he struggled to close the tiny clasp.

"I think I know who is getting married, Garrett." She pressed a finger to the heart.

"Do you, now?" His voice broke as he raised her left hand to his lips and gazed down at her with a fire in his eyes.

She tried to keep from grinning. "Since you told me this was your mother's, I'm guessing your father is marrying…"

"That's the guess I get from that good kissing? I'd hoped I'd scorched some sense into you." He reached into his pocket and pulled a ring from his pocket.

When he slid down onto one knee, she pressed her hands to her mouth. He made a face of exasperation as he grasped her left hand. "Got my mother's ring back today from the jeweler."

His mother's ruby engagement ring had been too large and he'd taken it to be resized for her. "I love it. I love you."

"I love you too much for us to delay this wedding any longer than we have to." Garrett stood and rubbed his jaw. "Can't believe you didn't guess after my kiss. Maybe we better work on that."

"Yes."

"Another kiss?" He embraced her but she held her head away.

"Yes to something you asked."

"You already said yes to marrying me." He tried to kiss her but again she pulled away.

"Yes, I'll go to the Lumberjacks' Ball with you. And yes, again."

He arched an eyebrow at her. "And the other?"

"Why, Mr. Christy—I wouldn't miss that wedding for the world!"

"I reckon you better not." Garrett's fervent kiss and close embrace held promise for a future she'd never imagined.

Thank God, the Lord had a better plan for her life—for life together with Garrett.

Chapter Nineteen

St. Ignace

Rebecca's hands trembled as she and her soon-to-be husband stepped to the edge of the dance circle. The performers tuned their instruments, in particular the fiddles, as everyone prepared for the first set to begin. But after all was done with the dance—her life would just be beginning, anew.

"Those gals look pretty as a bunch of spring flowers," Garrett proclaimed, as he swept Rebecca into his arms for their first dance of the Lumberjacks' Ball.

Sure enough, the dozens of young women from town who'd purchased fabric from both Rebecca and the Labrons, now wore beautiful creations, many made by Sister Mary Lou. "You're right, Garrett. They're so colorful and lovely. There are pink silks, blue satin moirés, and lots of yellow, too." The Labrons had a sale on a bunch of bolts of yellow brocade, which they'd over-ordered.

Soon she and Garrett were whirling around the packed-dirt dance "floor." Was her breathlessness from dancing or was it because of what was ahead tonight? She would become Mrs. Garrett Christy in a matter of hours.

She followed Garrett's gaze to where Pearl and Frenchie stood.

"Pa outfitted them and the grandkids with some new clothes."

All wore some shade of red and navy. Even the tiniest boy sported a navy vest with matching trousers and a bright red shirt. Pearl and Frenchie were doing well with the children—but they were getting old. And they'd accepted that Garrett and Rebecca would be waiting in the wings if they ever needed help. And they'd agreed to move to Mackinac Island with them.

They laughed as Frenchie hoisted Jimmy overhead and twirled him around.

What would it be like to help raise these orphaned children? "We should watch the kids and let Pearl and Frenchie dance a jig or two." She hesitated in following his lead, but Garrett continued to hold her in his arms and spun her around.

"Nah, Pa and Richard have that all under control." Garrett pulled her closer. "They're gonna spell them for a bit, later."

"Spell them?" Rebecca frowned at him.

"Give them a break. It's an Appalachian saying."

"If you say so."

"Just did." The music stopped and he released her and looked into her eyes. "You're staring at me."

Her cheeks heated. "I. . . I'm just thinking about later."

Garrett's face turned a little red. Maybe that was from someone tossing more wood into the nearby fire, though.

Woodsmoke rose, the scent tickling her nose.

Her beloved looked like he was about to say something to her when a local journalist tapped his arm.

 C3E0

"The Lumberjacks' Ball is turning out to be the event of the season." The newspaper reporter scribbled notes on his pad of paper as Garrett escorted him around the cleared camp site.

Lots of shanty boys had cleaned up so fine that Garrett would never have guessed they made their living working in the woods. "Must be over a hundred people here."

"At least," the man agreed.

"I know I've not seen so many beautiful ladies all in one place in all my live-long life." Garrett tugged at his tie, feeling more nervous than he had in his entire life, also. He was about to become a married man. There was one woman, though, who outshone all the rest.

"I have it on good authority that there will be a private wedding afterward. Do you know who the happy couple happens to be?" The slim gent, attired in a broadcloth suit cocked an eyebrow.

Garrett grinned. "I'm not at liberty to say. It is private, as you just said."

The journalist pointed to Sister Mary Lou. "I see the nun from the orphanage is here. I heard that she actually sewed most of those fashionable gowns the town ladies are wearing."

Nearby, a group of townswomen clustered, their upswept hair and bustles all perfectly in place. No two wore the same hat. They sure were a right purty sight.

"That's correct. Do you know Sister Mary Lou?"

"No, but I'd like to interview her."

"Sure thing. Come on." Garrett led the younger man over to where the nun sat at on a bench at a split log table, sipping fruit punch. She looked plum wore out—probably from putting last minute flourishes and fancies on the ladies' gowns.

As far as Garrett was concerned, the only fancy thing his Rebecca Jane needed now was a wedding ring on her finger.

ೞ

"Won't Garrett be surprised when you change out of your dance dress and into a wedding gown?" Jo Christy grinned conspiratorially as Rebecca and she carried the beautiful gown into Richard's cabin.

"I think he will." Rebecca giggled like a schoolgirl. "I'm glad we kept the wedding gown a secret. Sister Mary Lou, Cordelia, and you did a wonderful job on this dress." She ran her hand over the skirt's silky fabric, reveling in its feel.

"Oh, he has a little secret, too." Jo arched her eyebrows.

"He does?" What was Garrett up to now?

A loud knock startled Rebecca and she squealed.

"Folks is clearing out, gals." Richard Christy called through the door. "I'll come back when they're gone."

"We better hurry." Josephine began unbuttoning Rebecca's dress down the back. She took care with the small bustle and the hooks and eyes holding her lace overlay in place.

Rebecca kicked off her brown pumps, ready to slip her feet into the new creamy leather shoes that matched her wedding dress. The Labrons had supplied the beautiful footwear at no charge. They were so sweet.

Another knock sounded. "Reckon you might need the bouquets and all." Mr. Christy, Garrett's father, was supposed to bring the flowers earlier but had forgotten until Jo had reminded him.

"Thanks, Pa. Leave 'em on the bench for now."

"Will do."

Soon, Rebecca was fully dressed in her wedding gown.

Jo took two steps back and gasped. "You look beautiful."

Rebecca moved to where Richard had a mirror propped against the wall. The kerosene light in the cabin glowed beside her as she stared in amazement. With her hair looser and wispy curls around her face, she glowed with happiness.

Maybe the flush on her face was from all the dancing at the Lumberjacks' Ball. But probably not.

Who knew that the boy who'd saved her from certain death, in the water, would become the love of her life?

God knew. And the hope He'd given her deepened her trust in Him, come what may.

A new tea shop with a tearoom, the love of a good man, the joy of the sharing in raising those delightful children who'd been orphaned—and a move to beautiful Mackinac Island. She couldn't have asked for more.

"Are you ready?" Jo handed Rebecca her bouquet.

Her parents weren't there, but soon she'd be part of another family and joined to her husband in holy matrimony. "Yes. I could not be any more ready."

Someone knocked on the door. "Reverend Jones says he's ready," Garrett's father called through the door.

Jo opened the door and Mr. Christy stepped inside.

"Rebecca Jane, I'd be right honored if you'd allow me to escort you down the aisle since your own pa ain't here."

Tears pricked Rebecca's eyes. "Thank you. Yes."

Jo rolled her eyes. "See what you've done? You've gone and made her cry."

Rebecca blinked back the moisture. "I'm all right."

Pa, for that's what she'd call Mr. Christy from now on, took her arm.

The big man grinned. "Let's end this Lumberjacks' Ball in a way none of us Christys will ever forget."

"You danced your first dance tonight as Miss Rebecca Jane Daggenhart, but your last dance will be as—"

"Mrs. Garrett Christy." She liked the way that sounded.

And as the introductory fiddle music for the wedding commenced, Rebecca took her first steps to her new life.

Mr. and Mrs. Garrett Christy of Mackinac Island—she liked the way that sounded *even better*.

The End

Acknowledgements

First, I want to thank God the Father, Son, and Holy Spirit; every book is for you! Thank you to my husband, Jeffrey, and my son, Clark, for bearing with me as I wrote this book. Also, thank you to Jackie Croteau Williams, my cousin by marriage, for her input, especially as to some of her family's history during this time frame and about stories she'd heard. Jackie has since gone on to be with the Lord, since this book first released.

Thank you, Debbie Lynn Costello, for help as critique partner for the entire project and Vicki McCollum, too, who joined us later. Thank you to my Pagels Pals Readers and Reviewers Group on Facebook. I don't deserve the blessing of their support, but God has blessed me with them regardless! Thank you to my first line Beta readers Regina Fujitani and Bonnie Roof (both of whom have joined the Lord in heaven), Tina St. Clair Rice and my other Beta readers, Angi Griffis, Rosemary "Chicki" Crawford Foley, Britney Adams, and Gracie Louise Yost. Big hugs to blogger members Nancee Marchinowski, Anne Payne, Kathleen Belongia, Debbie Lynne Costello, Sonja Hoeke-Nishimoto, Cheryl Baranski also a resident of heaven now, and Debbie Mitchell. Thank you to Sister Mary Lou Kwiatkowski (who let me borrow her name!), Libbie Cornett, Wendy Shoults, Susan Floyd Fletcher, Chris Granville, Kathleen L. Maher, Maxie Lloyd-Hamilton Anderson, Betti Mace, Nancy McLeroy, Martha Phillips, Ann Lacy Ellison, Caryl Kane, Lisa Stifler, and Jean Kropid.

Thank you to Narielle Living for editing the original novel. Much appreciation to Sherry Moe who read for line edits on the 2022 version and to Susan Johnson who also read this newer version. Any errors in the book are my own.

Thanks to my former Overcoming with God "angels" who got drafted into my reviewer group Diana Flowers, Noela Nancarrow, Teresa Mathews and Bonnie Roof. A "shout out" to the Facebook 1K1HR group, Facebook CIA group (in particular Valerie Comer and Jan Edttii Thompson), and my former accountability partners Melanie Dickerson, Sarah E. Ladd, and Julie Klassen.

Author's Notes

Michigan's Eastern Upper Peninsula was becoming a busy place at the turn of the century. Although I grew up there, I still learned new things while researching this story. As mentioned, Jackie Williams and I enjoyed talking about Michigan's history, particularly about the resorts that were built there during the 1890s.

Thank you to the Fort de Buade Museum in St. Ignace, Michigan, in particular for their website and for the wonderful historical pamphlet they produced. St. Ignace has an amazing history and was a busy place in the 1890s. I love the straits of Mackinac, with the three main areas of Mackinaw City, Mackinac Island, and St. Ignace. It is a beautiful area. The Michigan State Parks are a great place to visit when you are there and offer many historic programs.

The inspiration for the change in this story, originally a "sweet" romance, was a song I'd heard online when researching lumber camps and lumberjack music in the 19th century. The horrid song was about a murderous lumberjack who went to a young lady's house, urged her to come out with him, takes her to the river and kills her. I was so shocked that someone would actually make such a heinous song, that I gave my story a twist with a young woman surviving such an attack.

Lumberjacks' Balls might also be called Woodmen's Dances or Woodcutters' Balls, but regardless, a dance where the lumberjacks could enjoy themselves would be a rollicking time. The town of Newberry, Michigan, where I grew up even has a Woodcutters' Ball that just took place in March, in conjunction with the Tahquamenon Logging Museum. If you ever get up to the area, be sure to stop in at the museum, which is filled with lumberjack paraphernalia and equipment. And you can even pop by and look into the log cabin where my grandmother, Maude Carrie Williams Fancett, grew up, as it is onsite!

There are many legends about Mackinac Island. This was the spiritual center for the Native Americans who populated the entire Great Lakes region. I like to think they were worshipping God, but had different names than what we use. This area was heavily populated by the French, beginning in the 1600s, with a great many priests coming along with fur traders. You will see I tried to use some of the French surnames for the characters. A great many Scandinavian people came into the area to work in the mines as well as in the forests as lumberjacks. People speaking Finnish became common, hence my workmen conversing in their native language.

Author Bio

Carrie Fancett Pagels, Ph.D., is the award-winning author of over twenty Christian fiction books, including ECPA and Amazon bestsellers. Twenty-five years as a psychologist didn't "cure" her overactive imagination! A self-professed "history geek," she resides with her family in the Historic Triangle of Virginia but grew up as a "Yooper." Carrie loves to read, bake, bead, and travel – but not all at the same time!

You can connect with her at www.CarrieFancettPagels.com.

Mackinac Straits Lumberjacks Series

The other books in the series are: *The Fruitcake Challenge* and *Lilacs for Juliana*

The Fruitcake Challenge was recommended in *Woman's World* magazine as a Michigan Christmas read! It was also a Selah Award finalist and a Family Fiction long list finalist for Book of the Year as were the other two books in this series. *The Fruitcake Challenge* was an Amazon bestseller and also part of a Christmas collection that was #1 in Christmas Anthologies on Amazon.

You can find my other books, including many set on Mackinac Island or at the Straits of Mackinac on my website under the Books section.

Thank you for reading Book 2 in the Mackinac Straits Lumberjacks Series!

If you enjoyed this novel, a review is always appreciated!

www.ingramcontent.com/pod-product-compliance
Lightning Source LLC
Chambersburg PA
CBHW072230190626
46809CB00017B/1680